Secrets

Agent Provocateur

Secrets

A COLLECTION OF
EROTIC FICTION

PAVILION

To agent provocateurs everywhere

First published in Great Britain in 2006 by
PAVILION BOOKS
151 Freston Road, London W10 6TH

An imprint of Anova Books Company Ltd

Text © Anova Books Company Ltd, 2006
(an earlier version of *You Smell of Chocolate* ©
Katherine P. 2003)
Endpapers © Agent Provocateur, 2006

Publisher: Kate Oldfield
Typesetting and jacket design: Lotte Oldfield
Copyeditor: Stuart Robertson
Proofreader: Emily Preece-Morrison

A CIP catalogue record for this book is available from the
British Library.

ISBN 1 86205 720 6

Printed and bound by MPG Books Ltd, Bodmin, Cornwall

10 9 8 7 6 5 4 3 2 1

This book can be ordered direct from the publisher.
Contact the marketing department, but try your bookshop first.

Contents

PREFACE

*F*or a long time now, we have wanted to explore potential Agent Provocateur publishing projects, particularly since we first started producing our own online magazine Knickers Forever, and noted the large amount of public interest in the personal entries from the AP Girls in the diary sections.

Moreover, during the last ten years, our shop windows have become infamous for their frank portrayal of the most popular, and some rarer but no less piquant, sexual and sensual fantasies. We have explored a range of personal predilections, from voyeurism to illicit liaisons, from phone sex to fetish. It seemed only natural therefore that Secrets, one of our first compilations of erotic stories, explores all of these themes and more through an exciting selection of original work from some new and exceptional writing talent.

We hope it stimulates the 'Agent Provocateur' in you.

Joseph Corré and Serena Rees, 2005

THE QUIET ONE

*S*he's wearing the purple one today. The strap on the left never stays up. The other one's digging into the flesh at the top of her shoulder where it's soft, but the left one hangs loose. I don't know if she notices. God, just looking at that strap and I'm hard. I don't know if she notices.

Chloë's confident. And she should be, she's good. Better than me. She has... aspirations. Me, I'm just happy I've got a job at all. I think she reckons she might be head chef or something one of these days. It's funny really, her running about all efficient, yes chef, no chef, right away chef. She likes it, showing me up. I've been here a year and a half and I'm still peeling potatoes. But Geoff's always calling her over and there they are, huddled over a steaming pot while

9

she pretends not to notice him staring down her front. Once he actually dropped a big dollop of marinara sauce, a big blotch on her new white jacket and I swear he nearly started licking it off before he remembered where he was. And her eyes just staring at him. Like she was daring him to. *Come on you dirty fucker – if you're gonna do it then do it.*

But with me, I don't know. She's nice to me – you know in that way that people are when they know they can do it better than you. Just a hint of patronising, not enough to be offensive, just that little bit flirty, enough to give you ideas. And she's not even pretty, you know. But she has something – it's like she has the secret and she's not telling. Her eyes, dark, and the way she moves them around at you under those eyelashes, the way she holds her back so that her breasts sit like they're perched on a shelf, the way she tilts her head a certain way, and that smile – is she smiling at you? – it's there at the corners of her lips.

There are times though, there are those times when I just can't tell where I stand. She'll brush right by me when there's plenty of room to pass, she'll be across the room and overhear some pathetic joke I've made to try and charm the waitress and I'll hear her laugh to herself. If she's just stroking my ego it's almost as good as a physical touch. There are days... most days. I'm in that cubicle by lunchtime, and a split second later there's come dripping from my clenched fist that I'm wishing was her.

～

It's the middle of summer, and it gets fucking hotter than Hades in that kitchen. I'm standing in the doorway out to the car park, with an unlit fag hanging from my lips. Janice is talking up a storm next to me, laughing too loud and all the while stroking her throat like there's buried treasure under the skin. God, if only I could. Janice would be a goer, I know it. But... bloody hell, I'm trying not to stare but there she is, Chloë, with her back to me at the counter just inside, chopping up onions. Not a drop of perspiration on her except there, right at the nape of her neck, there're those dark soft hairs clinging to her skin like a jealous boyfriend. Then suddenly a drop skittles down into the warmth beneath her collar and her hand whips back to catch it and just a pause before she sucks it off her finger with a loud snap. And she's looking straight up at my reflection in the gleaming pot on the shelf above her. My mouth starts to water as if the sharp taste of her sweat was on *my* tongue and I have to use all my strength to turn back to Janice and flash her a smile as I light my cigarette.

Tonight's the big party – fifth anniversary of the

restaurant. It's going to be a nightmare, I can tell already. Geoff's running around like a Michelin star depends on it (he'd be lucky) and they've drafted in some extra waiting staff who look like their faces could be the inspiration for the bullshit fancy pizza they've got on the menu; barely out of nappies. But of course, there Chloë is, dicing, stirring, grating at every turn. She wanders out the back door just as I'm exhaling the last of my cigarette, and the butt hitting the ground matches my sinking feeling. Shit. I should've stretched it.

'All right Ben?'

'Mmm, yeah. Not bad.' I made a point of looking her in the eye. I wanted to see where this feeling was coming from, maybe I could cheat it.

'Ready for tonight?'

She was reaching round behind her to pull a packet of cigarettes from the waistband of her trousers and a gap appeared at the front of her jacket, a peek of flesh clad in purple lace. Then gone.

'Have you got a light, doll?'

I held the flame to her face and she moved closer to me. I could feel her making the air warm, moist from the heat she'd carried with her from the kitchen. She put both her hands around mine, as if to steady the flame. Was my hand shaking? The touch of her fingers felt like ice and then fire. But I kept looking at her. She lingered for a fraction of a moment, and then exhaled a dart of grey smoke, her eyes whipping up into mine. Then that smile, just at the corners of her mouth.

'All right. I'll see you in there, Chloë.'

⤚⤙

Three minutes past one. The last punters have finished their pretentious conversations over coffee and cognac, and the last of the spotty teenage waiters have been picked up by their mothers. Geoff and the owners are draining their fifth bottle of Moët at a corner table. We've got through a good few bottles of dessert wine and brandy in the kitchen and there's that orange hazy slow motion feeling in the air – candle-light, alcohol and, yeah, I suppose a job well done.

I'm sweeping a pile of peelings into a mound, trying to avoid Janice, who's been making eyes at me all night. She was wearing some kind of low-cut wrap-around dress that made me wonder if she thought she was a madam rather than a hostess. It was for my benefit, I know, and I admit she caught my eye for a second. Shit, I can't figure it out – I've got pussy being served on a platter and here I am wanting to work for it.

She had gone into the toilets, Chloë, getting changed out of her uniform. By the end of the night I had given up trying to hide the fact that I couldn't keep my eyes off her. She'd look up and there I was. But I wouldn't look away, and she'd carry on cooking, moving in my gaze. With that smile playing at the corners again…

⤚⟋⟍

'Ben?'

Fuck, did I pass out? Only for a moment. I'm sitting on one of the benches in the cloakroom area, where the uniforms are hung up. I'd taken off my jacket and I'd forgotten that I'd not worn anything underneath because of the heat. Chloë is staring down at me.

'It's always the quiet ones, I suppose.' Her voice sounded like she had grains of sand in the back of her throat.

'What? Shit, sorry – has everyone gone?' It was dark in here, and she was framed by the dim light from the kitchen just beyond. She was wearing a shirt, one of those fitted ones, and jeans that were too tight. I'd never seen her not in uniform. I suddenly realised I had an erection. She couldn't have missed it either.

'Your tattoo.'

'Oh. Yeah.' She stared down at my chest, then back into my eyes.

'What does it mean? Are you heartbroken?'

'Not broken. Bit sore I guess.' I don't know why I'd

14

got a fucking bleeding heart. It seemed like something noble I suppose. She stayed quiet, just standing over me. I could see her breathe, her chest moving in and out, tense, like a balloon about to burst. Finally she speaks again.

'I've got one too you know.'

'Where?'

She chuckled, the way she'd laugh to herself across the room from me.

'If you can find it…'

She stopped. Deciding whether or not I should be allowed to take it that far with her. Her head was lowered and her hair was in her face. Then after a moment her head sprang back and she shook it away like it was restraining her. She exhaled.

'If you can find it I'll do whatever you want.'

Her eyes are boring into mine, challenging me. *Come on you dirty fucker – if you're going to do it then do it.*

I made myself stand up before I could think about it too much. My cock was straining against the front of my trousers and I couldn't help feeling a bit ridiculous as I walked over to her. But no, all she would do was stare into my eyes. I was standing close enough to smell the faint tang of cigarettes on her breath. And then I move that fraction of a step closer and she lowers her eyes, just for a second. She looked away.

My hands feel like they're moving through drying concrete, I can't do anything fast enough. But the minute the tips of my fingers touch the skin on her chest where her shirt falls open, I'm hit by a rush of electricity so sudden I can barely see straight. Slowly. Yes slowly. I'm tilting her chin out of the way, so that V of skin can catch the light. Nothing. I edge the fold of her collar away at each side of her neck, peering down at her shoulders between the shadows of her clothes. There it is, the one strap of her bra digging in to her shoulder, the other one's hiding down in the sleeve of her shirt. I can feel my breath bouncing off her skin, our chests matching each rise and fall. She smells incredible, vapours of warmth are coming off her body and it's sweat and something else, I didn't know what it was but it was elemental, animal…

My fingers are at the buttons now, working slowly. It's open now, but there's no light to see her by. I slip my hands underneath the fabric of the shirt and onto her shoulders, and slide them down her arms until the shirt's hanging limp around her wrists, barely clinging on. She inhales a very small sharp gasp of air, like her breathing is caught for a moment. My eyes are roaming over every inch of her, but nothing. Her skin is smooth and taut and glowing. But nothing. I turn her toward the light, this way, that. I move around her, behind her now, I'm at her back, I trace my finger down her spine and she arches it even more coyly than usual. But there's still nothing there. Shit, and now I can feel blood pumping into every cell of my body, not just my cock but everywhere, because my fingers are skimming the top her jeans now, and the satin skin of her midriff spills ever so slightly over the band each time she takes a breath. I can't go slow anymore. My fingers are fumbling at the button, the buttons they're all buttons all the way down and then I'm peeling at her jeans, my body leaning into her, hunching over her, my chin on the strapless shoulder, looking down her back at the curve of her hips, God it's beautiful, her ass from that angle. I think I feel her tongue against my neck, just for a moment, but no, she won't move and I pull back and she looks at me again, stares into my eyes. *Come on...*

Her jeans are bunched up around her knees. Her thighs are big but they look strong, she has that line where the muscle is defined along the sides of them. I run my finger along the groove as though that might help me find something, and now I'm resting on my knees in front of her, poring over every inch, and her whole body is trembling and for a second I think I feel her strain her pussy ever so slightly towards my mouth but no she won't move because I can't find it, it's not there anywhere and I shuffle around her on my knees staring up at her soft dark pants that don't quite cover the folds where her ass meets the top of her thighs at the back God, I can't take it – where is it?

I'm back around in front of her and I'm still on my knees. She's staring down at me. And now my hand is at her left knee, gripping it, half-heartedly trying to lift it out of the jeans but she does it, her hands are on her hips and she won't stop looking down at me, she doesn't need to lean on me for balance, and both her legs are out of them now and there she is staring down at me with her hands on her hips in her purple bra and her cotton pants and that smile still at the corners. There we are, she's staring down and I'm staring up and she's won, she thinks. She's won. *You had your chance, you dirty fucker. Ha!*

And then I see it…

It's under her left arm; right up underneath in that sweet soft part. A small, black X. I can't stop the grin from spreading across my face, I think I'm going to burst but then I look up and its not there anymore at the corners, her smile. It's gone. And that moment, I know I've beaten her… Did I want it like this? I'm not sure.

But no, I have to. I stand up – really slowly, and all the time looking, watching, and now I'm looking down on her and her eyes can't hold my stare, she can only glance up at me and then down at her arm, which I'm slowly lifting up by the wrist, my whole hand around, it's around her arm. And then my mouth – my tongue, my lips, my teeth, everything I could offer – was against that spot, rough and angry against that sweet victorious spot, and I could feel her arm twisting round in the grip of my hand but I didn't let go and we couldn't keep our balance any more. She fell to the floor and it was hard but warm from the night air and the skin of her was against the skin of me but no they were in the way take off pull off rip off the bra and the pants and the trousers I could barely hold out but there I was, holding her down against the tiles (did it hurt? I don't know) she said whatever I wanted and yes she wanted it my God her pussy was so incredibly wet I could feel how wet against the tip of my cock and I had to stop I held her there for what seemed like a century until I couldn't I had to and I was inside her I was fucking her *hard* it felt like I went into her a thousand times and each time I can't understand it she could squeeze me from inside her my hands are on her hair it's tugging she screams and I pull out for a second and she groans I drag her up and bend her over she's leaning over one of the benches and yes like that from behind every sound she was making fuck every sound I couldn't –

Then air. Finally air. I almost feel like I'm going to suffocate but there, it's slowly moving into my lungs now, it's moving in slow like honey. Feels like the first

breath I've ever taken. I can't stay though. I want to –
I *have* to – take my cock straight out of her, and walk
away. Leave her there. But I can't move. She's… I can
still feel the aftershocks of her, she's tight, she won't
let me go. I feel like her whole body's wrapped around
me. It has to be now. Walk away. But I can't move.
Just can't.

No. I waited too long. She had me. And that smile
comes back to the corners of her mouth.

LET THEM EAT CAKE

*L*ook at them scurrying in. Ten minutes to spend £200 for a couple of hours' pleasure. It's so cheap, so predictable. Girlfriends, mistresses, sometimes even wives, blissfully unaware of the lack of thought, the lack of time their oh-so-busy partners have invested in selecting their 'perfect' present. It's a wonderful, wonderful shop. I look at it every day. I watch the women go in and come out transformed. But the men. Nine times out of ten they don't pay the place the respect it warrants. They're always on a budget. Not money, but time. They're running into the best boutique in London and they treat it like a fast food joint. Disgusting. They should be banned. They don't deserve to be served. Don't deserve to see the delights on sale in there. Don't deserve to see my Angel.

The women, though. They're different. Some of them have to run in during their lunch hours, but mostly not. And even the ones who do have usually been in a couple of times before, trying things on, asking for advice, getting measured by the pink princesses who work there. They might not buy it then, but they're back. They always come back.

Most of the women have time. Real time. Time to luxuriate in their own pleasure. They shop for their own pleasure, dress for their own pleasure, undress for their own pleasure. You can tell by looking at them. They discuss new product lines, they chat with the girls, they enjoy every aspect of the lingerie-buying experience. For them the thrill is as much in the choosing, in the imagining how they will look, and what they will do in the new set of bra, stockings and panties, as in the actual wearing. And it's the shop girls who set the scene, who give them the courage to explore their own sexuality, to try things for themselves and not give a fuck about anyone else. 'If he doesn't like it, there are plenty who would.'

I heard Angel say that. I try to take my cigarette breaks when I think she's between customers because often she stands in the doorway, chatting to people as they pass. Sometimes van drivers honk their horns at her and I wish them dead. I wish them wrapped around the next lamppost, their horns blasting unstoppably as a macabre reminder of their vile disrespect. Angel deserves better than that. She deserves better than builders whistling at her, men calling out hello from the other side of the street, taxis drivers pulling over to ask her directions to places they already know. She deserves better than all of this. And one day...

Working opposite Agent Provocateur didn't even register when I first got my job. The chance to do print work for the likes of Madonna, Oasis and Angie Stone – who'd say no? It suited me then, the long hours, the intense meetings, the over-commitment to impossible deadlines. And when everyone else went home, there was me to finish off. 'Elvis' the Colombian cleaner calls me. As in that fairytale, *The Elves and the Shoemaker*. I've never corrected her on the pronunciation; I quite like the way she makes both words rhyme. But I get her point. The rest of them clear off to their parties or their football at six, and I stay and get the job done for when they turn up the next day. It's been like that for four years now.

I've never minded the hours. But Sandra did. And then one day, when I got home at eleven for the third night running, there was a note. She'd gone. She didn't know if she'd be back. And she wasn't even sure I'd notice for a few days (she loved her sarcasm). But I should thank my boss for ruining my marriage.

That was six months ago. My childhood sweetheart, vanished. The girl who rescued me from my cage of incurable shyness and introduced me to the world. The girl who held my hand through the peaks and troughs of adult life for twelve years. Gone. Just like that.

So obviously I threw myself into my work. And it was then I started to notice the shop across the road. Obviously I knew it was there but Sandra wasn't into things like that. I know she would have hated me coming home with one of those provocative outfits they have in their windows. And I know I would have been too embarrassed to buy one. So I never took much notice of what went on.

But now I do. Now I see the staff arrive in the morning, I see them take their lunch and I see them leave. I see them all. But mostly I see Angel.

If I had to describe perfection a year ago, I would never have said it was 5'2" – 5'5" in work heels. I would never have dreamed perfection had dyed red hair down to her shoulder blades, sometimes worn in bunches or occasionally tightly pinned up in mock severity. I never would have imagined it to have such an obvious hourglass figure, perfectly exploited by (and, to be fair, perfectly exploiting) the cut of her tight pink shop uniform. Green contact lenses some days; thin, rectangular dark brown glasses others – neither would have entered my thoughts back then.

But now…

Some nights I work late just to catch up with the jobs I daydreamed through during the afternoon. From the most productive employee to the least in half a year, and that's saying something. Luckily for me everyone puts it down to troubles of the heart. And they're right. But it's not Sandra I'm pining for. Not at all.

It's 9.20. The D12 artwork is done. The Americans should be happy – I'll know by the time I get in in the morning. I collect my bag, flick off the lights and trot down the stairs to set the alarm. The numbers for the code are the boss's birthday – how vain is that? He reckons no one has an excuse for not buying him a present. The machine gives its annoying whine and I have 30 seconds to leave the building before the local police descend on the place (in theory). I slam the door shut with 26 seconds to spare, lock the double bolt and slip the keys into my pocket. As I turn to walk towards the tube I notice a flickering out of the corner of my eye. I stop and turn slowly. It's the shop. It's AP. Their window lights are crackling into life, throwing pink illuminations across the darkened street.

For a second I pause, confused. I've never seen action in there past eight o'clock. Is it burglars? I step back into the shadow of my office doorway and hook my mobile out of my jacket pocket. Now's as good a time as any to test the Soho police response time.

And there, in the window, movement. What's going on?

I don't believe it. It's her. It's Angel. Still dressed in her fantastic pink tunic dress and high stilettos, black to match her stockings, she steps up onto the display ledge carrying a small box.

What should I do? Should I look? Would she see me? Would she mind?

Rooted to the spot, I watch as Angel walks towards one of the mannequins in the window and stands next to it, hands on hips. She looks up at the model's face, its beauty spot just above the lip, the white powdered skin, the small eye mask held coquettishly on a stick, hair lost beneath an extravagant Louis XIV ice cream wig. She reaches round the back and slowly starts to unhook the exotic corset from this Amazonian woman. One. Two. Three. Four… With each fastener loosened, the corset gradually begins to slide and I see the dark ridge of nipple beginning to appear on each breast. And is it me, or is Angel excited by them too?

I've learned more about the French Revolution looking at this window display for the last month than I ever remembered from school. I've thought about it every night, with Angel as my history teacher.

The corset finally collapses its grip on the model's waist and slips to the floor. The amazingly pert, high breasts are perfectly placed for Angel's mouth should she want them. And I know she does. I see the way she looks at her girls, her customers. I see the thrill she takes from helping them with their straps, adjusting their front-fasteners, clipping in their suspender belt while knelt between their legs.

It's so dark here in the street. I'm so nervous of being seen, but I shouldn't worry. Angel is in control. She looks over at me and smiles. She's still smiling as she pokes out her perfect red tongue and draws it along the underneath of the model's breasts. One at a time, just dragging her tongue beneath each cup. She rests her hand on the model's waist for balance and that hand goes lower, exploring the perfect curve of her partner's inanimate cheeks, running her long, red nail against the thin, blue lace suspender. She looks again out of the window as she drops her hand into the tiny satin panties. She wants me to join her. She is showing me what she wants me to do to her. Inviting me.

Angel steps over to the next model, locked with a surprised expression in a Revolutionary guillotine. She's pinned on all fours, her perfect apple-round bottom directed along the back wall of the display, her breasts hanging beautifully down, her head locked tightly inside the wood of the stocks, her neck exposed to the shining, deadly silver blade poised dramatically a few feet above.

Angel unclasps the lock and without altering the model's position, moves her gently to one side. Then she kneels down in exactly the same place, lowers her head into the hollowed out groove and with her right hand reaches up for the wooden bar to lock herself into place.

She wants me to see her pink uniform rise up above her thighs, exposing her perfectly round, welcoming arse. She wears tiny shorts, made of red and black silk, with a bow at the top, but these, too, barely cover her magnificent cheeks. She wants me to see them, wants me to run my fingers around the curved line where they meet the top of her thighs, wants me to scoop them together in both hands and bury my nose in the dark line between them. Inhaling, exhaling. She wants me to kiss her, to lick her from the top, from the small of her back, down, down, down in a perfect arc to beneath, to where she's hottest. She shifts her knees. She wants me to be able to reach, without stopping, her wet pussy, as silky in its own way as the panties my tongue hooks underneath and moves.

She wants me to pull back, to stroke her bottom, to run my thumb down the line where my tongue has just been. Angel is very specific on this. She wants me to pull her silk shorts up high so as much of her flesh as possible is on show to me. She wants me to kiss her everywhere. Bite her, kiss her, nuzzle her, bite her.

All the while letting my hands caress the backs of her legs, running the short distance up from her knees to where the roundness of her cheeks appear, always careful to let my fingers drag slowly between her legs, dipping into wetness, teasing for a second, but not lingering. Just pulling through, stroking upwards towards the dimples in the arch of her back, to where I'm kissing. Kissing and biting.

Angel loves the red marks that appear on her alabaster skin. She loves the physicality, visualising her own pleasure, seeing her own body react as if detached from her mind. But tonight she can't see. In the shop window, reflected, she can make out me kneeling behind her. She can see her own face, her own hands, locked solidly in the grip of the machine. But she can't turn her head. She can see me raise my hand, but she can't see the perfect pink impression it leaves as it smacks her beautiful white flesh. I can't see her face, I can't see her mouth forming the perfect 'O' of surprise as the first slap lands. I can't see her mouth but I hear the short 'ooh' it emits, trying to sound in pain but revealing only to me her pleasure.

Again and again I bring my hand down until my original handprint is smudged by others, like childish butterfly prints on virgin white paper. Her large, firm buttocks move enticingly with each blow. They quiver, shudder in response, small goose bumps appearing under my touch as though she were cold. But Angel is not cold. The very opposite.

The lower I smack, the closer I reach to the tops of her thighs, the more she squeals, the more her mouth forms the 'O,' the more I punish her for the noise.

Then I stop. She enjoys it too much. Somehow Angel is in control, even locked in the unyielding wooden stocks, rapacious blade poised above her pale neck. Somehow she is guiding me, making me touch her where she wants me to. But Angel demands more than that from her lovers. She demands they dominate her.

So, just as her noises crescendo under my smarting touch, I stop. I stop, stand up and step back. She is naked to me, despite the clothes. She is vulnerable. She is there for my taking. My Angel has done this for me, offered herself to me.

Lowering myself to the side of her kneeling frame, I run my hand over the tightness of her bunched up dress, risen high up her back. Always tightest around the shoulder blades and waist, always struggling there to grapple with her large, round, soft breasts, to offer modesty where she would instinctively prefer none. Her arms are locked forwards, there is nothing to interfere with the profile view of her breast pushing downwards from the height of her tummy, distorting the cut of the pink fabric, imposing its own shape on the designer's limitations. I reach out and touch. Where her flesh is soft, this feels firm. There is little room to breathe.

I run my hand further, towards the neck elongated by the difficult pose, and feel my fingers trip over the collar on the dress, feel them reach an unbuttoned hole, and then dive onto the hanging smoothness of her skin. She wants me to slide my hand inside her top, to reach into her overfull bra, to lift her out, to release her from the repressive constraints of her uniform. So I do. Slowly, edging my hand deeper and deeper around her warm, melting curves, feeling the flesh move and spill around my fingers, I reach her nipple, imposing and erect, unbowed by my touch. I run my hand over it and feel it etching onto my palm, sharp and soft at the same time. And I hear her moan again.

Angel wants to see me. She wants to see what I do to her. But does she really? I reach behind to the pile of costumes and pull up a mask. It is black with dyed feathers spilling out, an eagle's beak, and covers just my eyes and nose. It is enough. She must not see her lover, not tonight. There will be plenty of time for this. Disguised, I manoeuvre myself around the imposing framework of the guillotine and stand before her. She stretches to look up, the struggle evident in her beautiful large eyes, dark brown today, peering up at me over her glasses. Her hair, bunched, hangs to the

31

floor. I wet my finger and run it along the thin steel blade of the deadly machine. I run it down the wooden column and along the solid beam that keeps Angel's head in place. And I run it over the back of her head, around past her ear, and to her lips. Her mouth is open, expectant. I trace my finger around the wet, warm red lips and feel her tongue come to meet it, to dance with it, to draw it in. She sucks my finger, the nail, both joints, up to the knuckle, all the time swirling her tongue around it, warm and welcoming, moving and inviting.

I know she wants more. But she must not see me, not tonight. So I stand up.

Angel squeals in surprise and disappointment but she stops when I raise my hand to her. Don't make me hurt you, Angel, even though I think you want me to. She drops her head lower and looks up pouting in mock contrition. She wants me to punish her. But I won't.

I return to the back of the display and admire the view once again. I know she can distinguish the general movements in the window, but can she know what I'm thinking?

I'm sure she does.

I kneel behind her raised bottom and once again allow my fingers to spread over the round whiteness, flicking under the silk that still clings on. With one hand I reach down and let her feel me near her pussy, touching everything around it but hovering for a second before making contact. I sense her tense in expectation. I sense her aware that where this hand teases, my other hand will not. I have unzipped my trousers and eased my hard cock out of my shorts and I enjoy stroking it, feeling its hardness in my hand, cradling it for a second, comparing it with the velvety softness below, where my other hand rests. I inch myself lower, widening my knees as much as my trousers will allow, and bend my cock forwards. For a second it hurts, the unnatural angle, the awkward pulling to reach its low destination. Angel's thighs spread slightly, but she too does not want to go lower. She senses what is to come. She senses the pressing roundness of my head sliding along the length of her pussy, dragging back and forth, brushing over her clit and covering it with her own juices. She senses the moment when I draw back slightly, and reposition, before pushing slowly upwards, inside. She senses her own flesh relinquish and be pulled in with my penetrating cock. And she wants to scream.

We stay like this, slowly locking and nearly unlocking, but Angel wants more. With the slightest movement registering a seismic reaction in both of us, she somehow manages to pull her bottom forward, then plunge it back. Pull forward, plunge back. I try to stay still, my hands resting on her waist, and she moves. I feel every inch being coated in her hotness, again and again, as she slides on me and off me, on me and off me, faster and faster.

In the shop window I can see her breasts swinging and I want to touch them. I lean forward, resting my chest on her back, place one hand on the floor and reach underneath. I don't grab, just let her exposed nipple rub over my hand again and again like before, but more urgent.

She is making noises I have never heard before. I let my hand drift from her breast and towards her thighs. So soft, so yielding to my touch, but sticky now, sticky with the juices slipping down from above. I reach back further and feel my own cock, burning at the touch, aroused more than I have ever felt it, and I feel her pussy pulling it in. I pull my fingers forwards and Angel cries. Her clit, so swollen and flushed, responds to my passing touch and I feel her pussy grip me tighter. I spread my fingers either side of my cock, straddling her clit, and hold still, allowing her to move against me just as she moves to fuck me. So still I remain, because that is what Angel wants. She wants to feel in charge. But I have the power.

Back she pushes, forward she pulls, grinding herself on me, grinding herself against my hand. The noises she makes are like a new music to me, unheard but never forgotten. As the music gets louder, her movements get more anxious. She's bucking now, hammering backwards, shuddering forwards, frantically, desperately, amazingly...

She comes with a noise that I think could rouse even the mannequins. It rouses me. Hearing her begin to sing her climax, this song of pleasure, triggers a response in my cock and I explode. I could not stop if I tried. A burning, sensational, soul-destroying burst of pure pleasure washes over me and for a second I'm blind, I have no focus. Nothing from the outside world enters my consciousness, it's all from within. The colours, the shapes, the sensations, the sounds, all come from within. From within my cock. From within Angel.

I fall backwards, fall against the wall, slumped and devoid of thought.

Everything is blank.

In front of me, across the street, I see Angel add the final touches to her circus display. She looks over at where I lay. Can she see me? I don't know.

YOU SMELL OF
CHOCOLATE

'Penny,' says my Master, patting me gently. 'Time to get up.'

I ignore him. I used to obey every command at first, but by now I know there is a lot I can get away with. Plus I like it when my Master is just a little bit angry.

'It's amazing how still you can be in the morning, considering the amount of fidgeting you normally do... isn't it, baby?' He kisses me on the nose. 'Come on, now. I want my coffee.'

'Make your own,' I say, my voice groggy with sleep. This earns me a sharp smack.

'It's ten. You've slept for ages. Get up *now*, and make that coffee.'

'Hmmm,' I say, turning round and burying my head under a pillow. 'Wanna sleep.' He starts to tickle me. I laugh and kick. He tells me to 'get up this instant or else'. I say 'no, no, *no*.' I am fully awake by now. I try to tickle him back. He grabs my wrists, and soon has me pinned to the bed. He bites me playfully, on my nose, my ear, then tickles me until I shout, between giggles, 'OK, OK, I'll make the coffee. Stop, please, *stop!*' We go through this ritual most mornings. I make the coffee. Fresh orange juice and buttered toast too. I bring this to my Master, who is sitting at his desk, reading his e-mail. 'Thank you, baby,' he says, without taking his eyes off the screen. It annoys me not to have his full attention, so I put the tray down with purposeful carelessness, and some of the juice spills. He does not seem to notice. I start to walk back to the kitchen, but my Master points to a piece of paper by his side.

'Today's instructions.' I read as I eat my breakfast:

Shave legs, shower, wash hair, brush teeth.
Pigtail. No make up, no perfume. Talcum powder.
Green dress. Girly knickers. No bra. Sandals.
Writing today — no disturbing me.
Go to shops — milk, paper, anything else you can think
of. Salad for lunch. Make in advance — going to fuck
you before lunch.

Secrets

Be in bedroom at noon. Dress on. Remove sandals and knickers. Handcuffs and black paddle on bed.

'Not the black one!' I think. The black paddle is made of rubber. It's long and thin, and really stings.

I follow my Master's instructions. By noon I am in the bedroom, clean and barefoot, my hair braided. I enjoy the sensation of my skin against the fabric of the dress – the only item of clothing I'm wearing.

There is salad in the fridge, ready to be eaten, and I have placed the handcuffs and the paddle on the bed. I bought the milk, the paper, a box of cereal, and some lettuce.

I have done as my Master asked, but have committed a small crime: I came back with my shopping in a plastic bag. My Master likes me to use a reusable bag instead – more environmentally friendly – but I forgot.

So I have hidden the plastic bag in the bin, covering it with rubbish, hoping he won't notice. This is a crime too: if, for whatever reason, I use a plastic bag, I then have to recycle it.

My Master walks in, and kisses me.

'Lie on your front, with a pillow under your tummy.'

I do as I'm told. My Master handcuffs me to the bed. I feel his hand on my bottom, then a smack, and another. He kisses my head, my ear, and slides his other hand up my dress, to feel my breasts. He squeezes one of my nipples, but not so hard that it hurts.

I am wet, and want him, but know I will be spanked with the rubber paddle first. I am not frightened – in fact the thought turns me on – but I am aware that once the paddling starts I will hurt so much I will immediately want it to stop.

I am spanked daily, usually by hand, sometimes with a paddle, crop, or cane. Most of my spankings are not punishments: my Master simply spanks me because he likes to. If I misbehave, however, he will punish me, and punishment spankings hurt much more – the crop or the cane tend to come out for those.

My Master feels my bottom through the fabric of the dress. He slides his hand in, and I feel a finger pressing lightly against my butt hole, stroking my clitoris, entering me. Then the spanking begins.

I'm allowed to keep my dress down at first, as my Master slaps me fairly gently with his hand, to warm me up. This doesn't hurt much. In fact, I'm enjoying myself, and getting rather wet. After a few minutes, my bottom feels pleasantly warm and tingly. I notice it especially when my Master pauses to pick up the paddle.

I feel the paddle against my bottom. My Master just holds it there, then pats me gently a couple of time. He gives me the first hard smack, and I cry out. Ten more follow, in quick succession. The dress is lifted up, and ten more smacks land on my now bare bottom. I let out little cries, and wiggle trying to avoid the blows, but I know it's not in my interest to resist.

'Stay still,' says my Master, accompanying this with a particularly vicious smack.

I scream, and do my best to keep still.

'I'm going to spank each cheek for a minute,' he says. 'Then you'll get another minute across both cheeks, and an extra blow at the end for every time you move.'

This really hurts, as the same area is spanked over and over. I squirm, cry, and, despite myself, wiggle.

'No moving.'

I try my best. By now I really hurt, but I'm also getting used to the pain, and am so aroused that I'm not sure anymore whether I want the paddling to stop.

My Master says I moved at least eight times, so at the end of the three minutes eight hard smacks with the paddle land on my already very sore bottom.

'Almost finished,' says my Master, patting me gently. 'Ten more for being such a lazy little slave this morning.'

I receive ten hard smacks in quick succession. Then my Master gives me a quick hug, and a kiss.

'That's it, baby. Unless you have anything to confess.'

'I don't.'

'You sure?'

'Yes.'

'Good. I'll fuck you, then.'

My bottom stings as I sit down to eat lunch. My Master blows me kisses across the table.

'I'm going to be working some more this afternoon,' he says. 'What would you like to do while I write?'

'Can I go to the cinema with Lisette?'

'Yes, go, but no ice cream or pop corn, and be back by seven.'

I nod, happy.

The film is amusing, but predictable. Lisette and I go to a coffee shop afterwards. She's argued with her flatmate and wants to be distracted.

'Tell me something juicy. You always have crazy stories to tell. Did he spank you today?'

'Oh, yes,' I say, sipping my hot chocolate. 'He may well spank me again for drinking *this*. He said 'no ice cream or pop corn.' Do you think hot chocolate counts?'

'Doesn't look like ice cream or pop corn to me.'

'I'm supposed to interpret his intentions. He probably doesn't want me to spoil my appetite.'

'Doesn't it piss you off sometimes? It's your business what you eat or drink.'

'My life is one big kinky game. What's there not to

like? I could say 'game over,' but it would only spoil the fun.'

'I'm sorry. You know I don't object. Freedom to do what you want with your life. Even if it involves a reduced hot chocolate consumption. I just wondered if it ever gets to you.'

'I have my rebellious moments,' I say, sipping the chocolate. 'And I enjoy how they tend to get me into trouble.'

'Tell me what he did to you today.'

'He paddled me,' I whisper. 'Handcuffed to the bed. Then he gave me this really hard fuck. He kept pulling me by the pigtail. I love when he does that. You know, so I have to arch backwards and it's easier for him to kiss me.'

'Oh, yes. Even good, old vanilla me likes that.'

'He said he would slap me on my face the moment I'd come. Which made me come faster. It's very intense when he does that – an explosion of pleasure and pain.'

'Does it distract you from the pleasure?'

'No, it makes it stronger. When I come, it's as if I'm falling. A sudden blow propels me up again, ready for a bigger fall.'

We finish our hot chocolates and walk through the park. I enjoy the cool evening air.

'It's almost seven,' I say. 'I better run home.'

The house smells pleasantly of oregano. There is tomato sauce on the hob and my Master is kneading dough, his hands covered in flour.

I go to cuddle him.

'Here you are,' he says, without returning the hug.

'You making pizza!'

'Yes, I am, but I'm afraid you won't be having any tonight.'

What? Then I realise: no, no, no, the bag – he must have seen it!

'I'm so sorry about the bag,' I say, hugging him. 'Are you mad at me?'

'Baby, I was only joking. Which bag? You smell of chocolate.'

Uh oh.

A few explanations later, I am bent over the table, the pizza dough in front of me, resting in a bowl covered in damp cloth. (I might get to eat dinner afterwards, but only if I behave impeccably.) He taps me with the rolling pin.

'Aw!' I say.

'That didn't hurt.'

'No, sorry, awed too soon.'

He hits me again.

'*Aw!*' I say, and this time I mean it.

He lifts my dress, exposing violet, frilly knickers.

'Very pretty,' he says, placing the rolling pin on the table and slapping me with his hand a couple of times.

I can hear him behind me, opening a drawer, picking something up, putting it back in, picking something else up.

He pulls my knickers down. They fall between my ankles.

A blow lands on my left buttock. It stings, but I was prepared for worse. Feels like a wooden spoon.

'A minute with this,' says my Master. 'To warm you up.' The 'warm up' is meant to be for my benefit – as I get spanked, I get aroused and, as I get aroused, I am able to tolerate more pain – but it's rather painful in itself and I'm tempted to ask if I can forgo it.

I don't ask. He'd probably say no. I take it and do my best not to wiggle. I am in no position to provoke my Master further.

The minute is over and my bottom is warm and tingly. I wish I could see what it looks like. It always turns me on to see my bottom bright pink. Often after a punishment I sneak to the bathroom and admire myself in the mirror.

My Master walks out of the kitchen. I stay in position, waiting for the punishment proper. I'm wet and long to touch myself. I press my crotch against the table.

'Close your eyes,' he says as he walks in.

I obey. I can hear him place some objects on the table. He blindfolds me with a black cloth.

There is a squishing noise: lube coming out of a tube.

I can soon feel soft, lubricated plastic pressing against my butt hole. It's a sensation I enjoy, but I am always a bit scared when I know my bottom is going to be penetrated.

My Master pushes the butt plug in. Very slowly. It's not that big, just a little fatter than a finger, but it's impossible to forget its presence. Not that I would want to.

'I'm going to hit you ten times with the rolling pin to start with,' says my Master. 'For drinking the hot chocolate. I'll show some mercy since my orders were ambiguous.'

Mercy? It bloody hurts. Only two blows so far and already I wish I hadn't had that hot chocolate. I do like how the blows sink the butt plug in though: it's as if I'm being arse fucked and beaten at the same time.

I bring my thumb to my mouth, not quite sucking or biting it, just holding it near, as my Master delivers another blow.

'Palms on the table,' he says. 'And stick your bottom out more. I'm not impressed with your position.'

I do my best.

'Ready?'

'Yes.'

Another blow lands on my bottom.

I place a hand on each buttock.

'Please,' I say. 'Hurts too much.'

'Come on, Penny. I'm not hitting you hard.'

'It's a rolling pin!'

'There is worse to come.'

'Can I have a break at least?'

'You just had one. Hands back on the table. Take it like a good girl or you'll only get more.'

I focus on my clitoris, pulsating with pleasure, and on my cunt, desperate to be touched and filled. I focus on the sensation in my bottom and prepare myself for the last six blows with the rolling pin.

They feel wonderful. Painful, but just right, just what I can cope with and long for.

'Well done,' says my Master, stroking my hair. 'You all right?'

I nod.

'Ready for the cane?'

'Yes.'

He rubs my sore bottom and tickles my clitoris from behind.

'You look so fuckable,' he says.

'I feel so fuckable.'

'How many strokes of the cane do you think you deserve for forgetting to bring a bag to the supermarket?'

'Four?'

'And for hiding the plastic bag?'

'Eight,' I say, and immediately regret it.

'All right, twelve with the cane it is,' says my Master. 'And then we can have a different kind of fun.'

It's a middle-sized cane. Used skilfully it won't open the skin or do any real damage, but it *will* sting and leave me with a stripy bottom.

'I'll cover you up for the first four,' says my Master, pulling my dress down.

I check my hands are well placed and get up on my tip toes, which makes my bottom stick out more. I listen for the noise of the cane, as it swishes trough the air and lands on my bottom.

As usual with canings, there is a time delay before the pain hits. It's a localised, burning sensation. It continues to sting intensely for about half a minute, then it fades.

My Master waits, letting me savour the pain. Eleven strokes to come, but I am not afraid. Endorphins are running through my body: I'm high on pleasure and pain.

He delivers a second stroke of the cane, with a quick, expert movement of the wrist. He is careful not to hit the same spot. Not yet, anyway.

I let out a gasp as the pain of the second stroke kicks in.

Another two, slowly paced, and my Master lifts the dress up. He places a hand on my bottom.

'Can I touch myself for the last eight?' I say, pressing my clitoris against the table. 'Please, I want it so badly.'

'It's a punishment, remember,' he says with a little hand smack. 'We'll see about pleasuring you later. Your stripy bottom looks very inviting.'

The last eight canings, without the protection of the dress, are more intense. The very last four particularly so, as my Master delivers them at a different angle, so they intersect the parallel stripes already decorating my bottom.

I let out a scream as the pain of the last stroke sinks in.

My Master unzips his trousers and takes me his hand finally on my clitoris. I reach the first orgasm fast. My anus contracts as I come and the plug falls out.

My Master squeezes lube on my butt hole. I am going to be arse fucked. That always makes me come like crazy. I smile, anticipating the pleasure, while he grabs my sore cheeks and parts them wide open.

AFTER HOURS

*D*an and I had been working on the same design project for over two weeks. It had been quite a simple brief, but was turning into one of those jobs that just won't die. Every time we had thought it was finished, the client demanded new amendments, and it was dragging on and on.

Only if I'm honest, I didn't really mind from the start. I didn't ever plan anything to happen, absolutely I didn't, and I can't even pretend I was going through a rough patch with Matthew. All it took was a rough phone call, actually, and very bad self-discipline, and a little bit too much red wine, to threaten three years of marriage and good intentions.

It was the last fortnight in January, the worst time of the year: no Christmas parties to look forward to, no time off work or excuses for new shoes; just an endless stretch of bad weather and dark nights. Towards the end of the month, my boyfriend's patience began to run thin. Understandably, he wanted someone to cuddle up to at home on these grim, cold nights. He wanted long baths and home-cooked suppers and frankly, so did I, only I was stuck at the office again. I think it was about half past eight on the last Wednesday of the month when he made that call. You know the kind: 'When are you coming home?' 'Yes but why?' 'Why don't you just leave it until tomorrow?' 'Why don't you tell them to shove it?' 'Why don't you outsource it?' He had had enough and who could blame him? Unfortunately there was nothing at all I could do about it, otherwise I almost certainly would have chosen not to be in that office on that night. Almost certainly.

By the time I got off the phone, I was pretty fed up. I knew that I had raised my voice and I wasn't very proud of it: even if I had been on my own it was fairly unforgivable to have spoken to Matthew like that. But I was full of wine and not a little sick of work. I was trying to get back into thinking about the layout on screen when a little icon pinged up in the corner of the screen with a tempting 'blip'.

Excellent reasons all. Next time please speak up so I can

borrow some of your explanations for my girlfriend.

I stared at the email and smiled as I realised it had come from Dan, not twenty feet away. Sweet. I guessed he was trying to get across politely that he had been forced to overhear my heated exchange with Matt, without making like a stalker.

Sorry about that. Just trying to explain that if we could outsource a job as easily as that, I wouldn't have one. Bless.

Understand perfectly. Perhaps we could outsource client. Or selves. Or perhaps we could outsource selves to off-licence and leave cleaner in charge?

I giggled. It was a long-standing, long-unfunny joke in the office that there was no cleaner. Our office looked glamorous, and there were always huge arrangements of fresh flowers in the window, but out of sight of the punters it was actually a little scruffy.

Before I could reply, a new message sign pinged up on the screen again:

Are you bored?

Yes, I replied.

Want to play scrabble?

Too tired. Vocabulary of newt.

Strip poker?

I let the message hang in space for a minute. Was he flirting with me? I threw a look at him but he was looking resolutely at the screen; I could only see his face in profile, but it was smiling.

No cards, I wrote feebly. Then, to try not make him feel rejected, I ventured jovially: *Spin the (empty) bottle?*

Have bottle, will travel, came the instant reply.

I thought for a moment, then wrote: *Spun virtual bottle. Is facing window. Boo.*

So am I, came the response. *Boo.*

I didn't understand it at first. I just stared at the screen. What does he mean? 'So am I' what?

Then I heard the chair squeak, followed by an odd noise. I craned my neck to look at Dan again, but I couldn't see him. Perhaps he was nipping to the bathroom. Perhaps.

I felt it before I heard him again. Something warm on my foot. I screamed and jumped back, terrified it was a mouse. Then I heard a chuckle, and a voice said softly, 'Boo,' but I couldn't work out exactly where it came from. I held my breath, afraid and confused for a moment. Then I felt it again, more decisive this time, and most definitely not a mouse. Without a shadow of a doubt, I felt warm hands run lightly from ankles along my calf muscles and back again, and hesitate for just a second, and I said nothing, nothing, and then again, such a light touch along my calf muscles and then over, under my skirt and stopping to rest on my thighs.

I didn't dare move.

'Call him back,' the voice said.

'Call who back?' my voice said, dumbly.

'Your boyfriend. Matthew, is it? Call him back. Make up'

'And say what?' I asked.

'Tell him you'll be home in an hour.'

'Will I?'

'How should I know?' asked the voice, and there were peals of laughter underneath my desk.

I could have done anything then. I could have been outraged. I could have screamed, and called security (we at least had security); I could have kicked out, or laughed it off, or anything. But I picked up the phone, and for reasons I don't fully understand, I called Matthew.

I was in the middle of apologising when it started up again. Fingertips, soft as night, began to inch higher up my thighs, under my pinstripe skirt. I almost froze, but I was mid-sentence, and I simply ploughed on. Loving and sincere on the telephone above my desk, and trembling like a leaf underneath it while unseen but very practised hands began more confidently to feel me up. Matthew was keen to smooth over our altercation and began to tell me about his day, the kind of small intimacies we would usually share over supper or relaxing on the sofa, while I let Dan, Dan who for some reason wasn't at his desk but was very clearly at mine, part my legs and snake his tongue, his tongue my God, along the inside of my thigh. I blushed a burning red as I felt his tongue bump over the ridge of my stocking tops (I know – who wears stockings to work?) and then his hands parted my legs wider still and I was sprawling and slipping lower under my desk while still perfectly respectably cooing encouraging noises and platitudes into the phone above it. And then I felt fingers moving across the oh so ticklish part of the crease of my inner thigh and then I shrieked into the phone and tried to disguise it – oh dear God – as a sort of sneeze to Matthew while Dan slipped his fingers into my knickers just long enough to catch them and pull them aside and press his tongue suddenly and hotly into my cunt. And now, oh I'm running so late, and ooh Matthew if you want me home anytime soon then yes I really must get on. I've still rather a lot to get through goodbye darling and Christ there is a hot mouth between my thighs and fingers pushing at my cunt and sliding in and this is fantastic and then the fingers withdraw slowly and gently and the hot mouth is gone and there is a grown man clambering out from underneath the desk and he asks me 'Sarah, Sarah what's with stockings for work?'

What do you say? I want to say a lot of things, obviously, but nothing came into my mind apart from 'Get back – why have you stopped?' and no doubt that thought is very explicit on my face.

Dan is grinning at me and his face is wet and I can smell myself on him and it is all wildly exciting. 'For Matthew,' I say, weakly. 'I wear stockings for Matthew. He likes it,' I offer by way of explanation. Dan has the grace to look a little crushed. 'Really?' he asks hopefully, and I begin to say, 'Of course–' but unfortunately I start to cough awkwardly and blush, also awkwardly, so that it is obvious even to the street-lamps outside that I am not entirely telling the truth.

Dan moves towards me and kisses me briefly and chastely on the mouth, and it is so sweet to taste myself on him I can't help myself and before I know it I am telling him. 'I like to,' I say in a rush. 'I like to wear them, and things, and think about rude… things, and it makes the time go quicker. Working.' What sort of things, asks Dan, and I say it. 'You.' There. It's out. I've said it. Now he'll know I like him, how embarrassing, and what about Matthew, only in retrospect maybe it's a bit late because this man's already had his tongue up me and I really would like him to do it again.

But of course, he's a man, and he wants to know details. He wants to be able to picture it, he says. What do I think about? When I put the stockings on that morning, before I put on my little suit and do my hair and make-up, what exactly am I thinking about?

And it's not Matthew, is it? Of course it's not. It's the grosser, just plain ruder side of me that wants to be forced to do delicious things just like this that I don't ever dream might really happen. 'Like what?' 'Oh, I don't know.' 'You do. Tell me.' 'Well, like kissing.' 'And?' 'Kissing... touching. Being undressed at work, weirdly, and touching you... kissing you... there...' (I'm gesturing embarrassedly) '... and doing it on top of the desk... usual sort of office thing,' I say brightly, and Dan is grinning from ear to ear. 'You fantasise about sucking me off,' he says, delightedly, and I'm blushing furiously now, and also suddenly nodding, and even though I can hardly ever be bothered to do this at home I really want to see Dan's cock now, I haven't seen a new cock in so long, and I want to put it in my mouth and see how it feels.

'Take your clothes off,' he says. He's not smiling anymore, but he looks friendly, still. Kind. He's scruffy, Dan, but he really has a lovely face, so he can get away with a lot. 'Take your clothes off,' he says again, louder this time, and I hesitate for a moment and then I think, ohfuckit, and I stare at him and take my jacket off. It's quite cold in the office because of the poxy air con, and I shiver a little, but he just looks at me and I reach round to unzip my skirt at the back, take a deep breath and just slide it off over my hips. I have narrow hips, like a boy Matthew says, and the skirt slips off easily and I step out of it and just kick it aside. 'Good,' says Dan, nodding approvingly. 'More.'

I don't want to take my shoes off because I am vain and I want my legs to look longer, so I simply peel off my knickers, which are kind of wet inside, one thing and another, and I bend down in what I hope is an alluring manner and pull them right down and off over my shoes, leaving me in stockings and shirt.

I feel like a teenager, half dressed and half not, and there is a dreamlike quality to what is happening. It feels very odd to be half-naked and so horny at work, but not wrong. My back is to the window, and Dan is sitting thoughtfully on my desk facing me, watching me, and I'm suddenly aware that I'm quite exposed to the world outside the window, just like in my fantasy. We don't have a cleaner, as I say, but I suppose other offices round here might, and they might see in, but actually it's coming up for nine now according to the clock, so it's just Dan and I, and the hum of the air conditioner in this bright, shiny, very very professional office environment.

Dan stands up and looks over my shoulder for a moment, and then he begins to unbutton my shirt. I thought he was calm, but I realise his hands are trembling, and his breathing is hard, which is oddly touching. He looks so cute in his glasses, so preppy and together, and yet the hard, friendly bulge in his carpenter jeans suggests another persona entirely.

He pushes the straps of my bra off my shoulders and then slips a finger into the lace cup of my bra, snapping it under my nipple but not completely uncovering my breast. I don't have large breasts, but they are very pert, and looking down I must admit they look nice like this. He does the same to the other side, flicking the nipple even further to attention and showing it off just a little, and then he stands back to admire his handiwork.

'You're quite lovely,' he says pleasingly. 'Will you get on your knees, please?' And before I can think of anything to say, he is right before me again, pushing me by the shoulders firmly down to the floor so that within moments I am kneeling on the rough carpet, my face buried in his groin. My boyfriend, Matthew, is an extremely courteous lover. He waits his turn and makes sure he pleasures me before we have 'real sex.' He does not stick his prick in my face, and so it is with a very guilty thrill that I find myself scrabbling at Dan's fly, pulling at his shorts and then pinging a surprisingly large, thick cock from its confines before nuzzling it with my nose and cheeks. I think again about the cleaners and the lights on in the other offices and then banish them from my mind as I begin to lick and kiss the tip of Dan's cock. Sliding one hand upwards to his belly I feel hard muscle, and a spasm of pleasure flickers between my thighs. I run my tongue down the length of him and back again, pleased by his moans, and he arches his back slightly to push himself further between my lips. He is so hard and fills my mouth utterly now, pushing quite carelessly at the back of my throat, and I breathe carefully so as not to gag and I rock gently, sliding my lips up and down as much of his cock as I can get in my mouth. I look up at him and his eyes are shut tightly, his own mouth an O of pleasure, before he opens them and we lock eyes while I carry on licking and sliding up and down him, one hand holding his firm ass for grip and also because it feels very nice indeed. Dan begins to moan louder and thrust a little more firmly for a moment, and then stops abruptly, letting out a long exhalation.

I don't know why he stops but I want to carry on.

Pulling myself to my feet I edge him gently backwards onto my desk, tugging his jeans to the ground and starting to straddle him, when my telephone rings and I am struck with panic, utterly grateful when Dan doesn't even flinch and orders me to answer it. I know I told Matthew I would be home by now but I don't care, and I reach for an excuse as I pick up the phone and Dan ducks down and takes a nipple gently between his teeth.

Only it's not Matthew, the voice. I don't know who it is, but his words make my skin tingle and my heart pound. Feeling me stiffen, Dan looks up quizzically, and then flicks the telephone onto loudspeaker.

'I can see you,' the man is saying. 'I hope you don't mind me watching, but it's a lot more interesting than my spreadsheets.' His voice is warm, with a gentle Scottish accent, and I realise that I am not afraid, even though I realise we could be fired for what we've done here tonight, and I do experience a moment's panic as I see for a momentary flash an image of myself, shamefaced; friends and family told, career in tatters; one of those urban tales for bored emailers. But the image melts. Dan is smiling at me tentatively, but looks a little nervous himself. 'I want to speak to your boyfriend,' the voice says, and I feel a little pang of guilt – not entirely unpleasurable – before nodding to Dan to go ahead.

'I just want you to finish off for me,' he says. 'Finish off as I ask and I'll leave you in peace.' I don't know how this man knew to call this number, and I wonder if he really can see us. I'm just thinking this when he says, 'Tell her I can see everything with her leant over like that,' and he murmurs appreciatively as I grow bold and exaggerate my position, thrusting my bottom out and widening my legs a little so he can get a really good look.

Dan looks at me. 'It's up to you,' he whispers, and he looks so concerned for me I want to kiss him. But I don't, because suddenly I don't want our guest to feel left out, and I lean over again and say with conviction into the phone, 'Tell us what to do.'

There is a moment's silence, and then the caller clears his throat. 'Bend her over properly,' he demands, 'right over the desk.' Without a word, Dan moves to one side so as not to obscure the window view, and tilts me over from the waist, so that my nipples graze the desk and my hips and buttocks jut out. My stockings are still intact, despite the rough carpet, but my knickers are on the ground so the crease of my cunt is clearly visible to both Dan and our guest. 'Show her to me,' says the voice, lower now and a little unsteady. Dan duly kneels down and puts his hands on my buttocks, holding me apart, and I feel a thrill of excitement to think that this mystery man can see my most private parts, a view of myself I have never seen. 'Touch her,' he orders, and Dan moves a hand down between my legs, stroking me gently for a moment and then pushing his fingers firmly and boldly deep into my cunt. Without being told to he begins pushing and pulling his hand to and fro inside me, groaning a little, and the man on the phone too sucks his breath in at the sight. My head is a rush from the odd position and I feel filthy but elated at the idea of these men staring into me, desiring what I have but unable to do anything much about it.

'Turn her round,' he breathes. 'I want to see you fucking her, sliding in and out of her.' Even as he speaks Dan is racing, grabbing me roughly and pushing me round to face the window, while he takes a seat on top of the desk. We tussle for a moment as he tries to position me, eager to please our mystery caller suddenly, and somehow liberated by the permission to show me off and objectify me, and I understand, and I feel freed by it, too. Dan sits me on his lap and opens my legs wide, then wider still, fiddling underneath me and then positioning his cock at the slippery entrance to my cunt. With a shove he slides the whole thing inside me, and begins to manoeuvre me up and down on his lap as though I were a doll.

'What do you think you're doing?' asks the Scottish man with a shocked chuckle. 'Don't you want her to enjoy it as well? Here' – he paused for a moment – 'I want her to play with herself. Finish it,' he orders. 'I want to see her make herself come.'

His words are barely out before I reach for my clit, grinning with delight, and Dan resumes his manoeuvring of me, leaning back slightly, his fierce stomach muscles holding out so he can catch sight of himself slipping in and out of me, while I open my legs as wide as I can, determined to help the caller enjoy the show. I lick my fingers unnecessarily, and feel a jolt of pleasure as soon as I touch my wet, yearning clit. I begin to rub it as gently as I can manage, teasing myself gently despite myself, but I know I am not going to be able to do this for long, and I lean back into Dan's arms. He is thrusting furiously below me, strong arms still moving me up and down, and I begin to gather speed, the feeling of pleasure between my legs spreading to my thighs, and I hear myself crying out. Dan wraps one hand around my breast and pinches a nipple, hard, and everything is suddenly all too much and I am hollering, a long, shocked wail filling the big room as Dan moves me fast and then slow until he almost stops, and I come hard, Dan still inside me rocking me gently, kissing my back over and over again. There is no noise now save for breathing, and I suddenly remember our 'guest' when I hear a friendly 'Goodnight,' followed by a click and a dialling tone.

There doesn't seem much to say. Going downstairs in the lift alone afterwards, I smile at myself in the mirrored panel, and I barely notice the rain slashing at my windscreen as I drive home still in time for supper. I know I should change jobs, I know it. But I can't help but think I'd rather keep my telephone number.

CINDERELLA

'Becky! Come in,' said Alma, opening the door. She was wearing a towelling dressing gown and a pair of slippers. Her long, black hair was dripping water on the floor.

'Sorry I'm late.'

'Ten minutes late isn't late,' said Alma. 'By my standards you're early. Glass of cava?'

'Please.'

Alma always stocks up on cava when she goes back to Spain to see her family.

'There you go,' she said, pouring me a large glass. 'Let's get ready. I'll show you what I'll be wearing.'

I was glad I was going with Alma. She always makes me feel braver.

I followed Alma up the stairs and into her bedroom.

'Like it?' said Alma pointing to a blue, sparkly dress laid out on her bed.

'It's beautiful. Much more interesting than my 'little black dress',' I said, pulling the dress out of my bag for Alma to see.

'I'm sure we can jazz it up.'

'Shall I change in the bathroom?'

'If you want,' said Alma, taking off her bath robe and throwing it on the bed. 'But it's more fun together.'

'I'll change here then,' I said, trying not to stare at Alma's full breasts, and taking a big gulp of cava.

I stripped to my simple black knickers and knee highs and started to put the dress on.

'Let me help you,' said Alma, now wearing a pair of white silk knickers and a matching silk and lace trimmed bra.

I turned round.

'You've got such a tiny waist,' said Alma, zipping me up. 'And a very cute bottom… All done,' she said, accompanying the remark with a gentle smack.

I jumped up in surprise. Was she flirting with me?

Alma put on a pair of white stockings, a suspender belt, the dress and a pair of blue stilettos.

She admired herself in front of her antique looking full-length mirror and started to apply mascara on her already thick, dark lashes.

'You look amazing,' I said, peeking behind her. 'I

feel a bit dull by comparison.'

'I haven't worked my magic yet.'

First, I let her do my make-up.

'You are like a doll,' she said, studying me, turning my face gently, as if she was about to take a portrait of me and was looking for my best angle, 'with your porcelain skin, your pretty little mouth, your huge Christina Ricci eyes...'

'Boys always tell me I look like a permanently startled deer. I'm not sure if they mean it as a compliment.'

'Oh, I think so. Startled deer are very attractive to predators.'

I sat at Alma's vanity table and studied my reflection. When Alma did her make-up, she tended to go for smoky eyes and deep red lips, but with me she had opted for a different style and pallet: a touch of green eye shadow, lip gloss, a little blush. I looked fresh and inviting, like a rose bud. I smiled to myself and turned round to face her.

She rummaged inside a drawer.

'Try this,' she said handing me a choker decorated with little crystals. 'And I've got just the shoes to match it somewhere...'

She got down on all fours, offering me a full view of her curvaceous bottom, and fished a pair of transparent plastic shoes out from under the bed.

'Far too outrageous for me,' I said.

'Cinderella didn't object! Come on, Becky, let me transform you for the ball!'

I held out a foot. I had no idea how I was going to walk on those shoes – and I'd look ridiculous – but I didn't want to stop Alma from doing her magic. On matters of style, she generally knew best.

'They fit,' she said. 'The prince will be pleased.'

We started to walk down the stairs.

I didn't get far.

I slipped and fell down two steps.

I sat on the stairs, holding my foot.

'I think I've sprained an ankle.'

'Oh no!' said Alma, sitting down two steps below. 'Would a massage help?'

'Please.'

Alma knelt on the stairs, taking the foot in her lap.

'Feels good,' I said, lying back and closing my eyes – and it did feel good.

I wish her hands would work their way up my leg, I thought – and immediately I blushed. To calm down I had to remind myself she couldn't read my mind.

Or could she? She gave me one of her wicked, feline smiles, the ones she normally reserves for desirable men, and her hands slowly moved up the leg, all the way to the knee.

I felt a wave of illicit pleasure, and there was no

denying it was sexual pleasure: my knickers were already getting wet.

Alma put a hand on my thigh. She held it there, delicately, and looked at me.

I attempted an inviting smile, then closed my eyes again, feeling foolish.

But she seemed to get the message and started to stroke my crotch through the fabric of my knickers.

'You are wet,' she said. And then: 'I don't think we should go to the party.'

Alma offered me an arm and we slowly walked back to the bedroom. I was both nervous and excited – I was going to have my first sexual encounter with a woman…

'Have you done this before? You know…?' I asked her.

'Yes,' she smiled, sensing my apprehension. 'Is this your first time?'

I nodded yes, blushing.

'I'll enjoy corrupting you, then,' she joked. 'Why don't you lie on the bed?' she said, patting the duvet lightly, indicating where I'd be best positioned. 'It's no good putting weight on that ankle…'

She opened the drawer of the bedside table. I could see vibrators and dildos (all in pretty shades of pink and purple), a large feather, a blindfold and a pair of handcuffs. My mind raced.

Alma reached for the black, silky, padded blindfold and put it on me. She handcuffed me to the bed, gently placing my arms in position.

She touched my lips with a finger. Her hair was tickling my face. She brushed it to the side and leaned to kiss me on the lips. The sensation of soft cheeks against soft cheeks, and soft lips against soft lips, was a pleasant surprise. And when our tongues met, I thought I had never enjoyed a kiss more. Perhaps girls were particularly good kissers. Certainly Alma was.

I could feel her breasts pressing against mine as she kissed me. I wanted to reach out with my hands, but they were tied over my head.

Deftly, she slipped my knickers off. I soon felt the light touch of the feather on my inner thighs, brushing my pubic hair, my outer lips. Then something wet and soft stroked my engorging clitoris.

'Your pussy tastes good,' she said.

She slid a finger inside my cunt and moved it slowly up and down, her tongue still teasing my clitoris.

I moaned and smiled dirtily as waves of pleasure rippled through my body. I'd had dreams and fantasies of lesbian encounters, but I never thought I would experience the real thing. I couldn't believe my beautiful friend was in bed with me, her finger deep inside me.

'Turn round,' directed Alma, freeing my hands.

Still wearing the blindfold, I turned onto my stomach.

She lifted my dress over my hips, exposing my bottom. She cupped a buttock with one hand, and with the other she reached for my clitoris, giving it a gentle massage.

She rummaged inside the drawer. She seemed to be undressing, maybe putting something on.

'Get up on all fours.'

I obeyed. I could feel soft lubed plastic pushing inside my cunt, Alma's hands on my waist. She started to move inside me, gently at first, then forcefully, pulling me towards her as she thrust deeper into my pussy.

'What's it like... being fucked by a girl?' she asked.

'Surreal,' I said. 'And wonderful.'

'Strap-ons are fun, but the next toy is even better...'

Alma told me to sit up, legs open. She sat opposite me. I explored her body with my hands. She had taken her dress and knickers off. I could hear her – and feel her – lubing another dildo. I touched it: it was thick and studded – and very long.

'Open wide,' she said, sliding it in.

She sat astride me and slowly mounted the glistening double dildo.

Sliding down, she stroked my clitoris and leaned in to kiss my lips then the nape of my neck, and nibble my ear lobe.

She grabbed the centre of the dildo and pushed it back and forth into our cunts, then we both started to thrust eagerly, greedily towards each other.

We kissed, thrust and stroked each other's clits until we both came, first her, then me, surprising myself by how loudly I was moaning.

'I'm all sticky ...' said Alma, with a glint in her eyes. 'I'll run a bath.'

We walked to the bathroom and got naked as the bath tub filled and the room got warm, steamy and scented with rose and jasmine.

Alma's bathroom was large, old fashioned and comfortable. The predominant colours were the white of the porcelain, the silver of the polished chrome fittings, and the blue and pink of her towels and furniture.

I got in first.

'Hey, central tap, that's convenient,' I said.

'Yeah, perfect for sharing,' said Alma, getting in at the opposite end of the tub.

I placed one of my feet on her mound. She looked up, smiling.

I raised my foot slightly to stroke her pubic hair, her outer labia. I pinched her clitoris between my toes.

I pushed the tip of my big toe inside her cunt, took it out and raised it to her mouth.

'Suck it,' I said.

'I knew there was a vixen in you,' she said, before obeying my order. Big toe at first, then as much of my foot as she could fit into her mouth.

I got hold of the shower-head, which rested on top of the central taps, and turned the stream on. I pointed it at Alma's face, who covered her eyes and laughed.

I smirked and quickly redirected the water towards her crotch. She adjusted her position, lifting her hips to the surface so the jet of water landed straight on her clitoris.

My foot moved towards her breasts, so soft yet firm and full.

I took my foot back and, still pointing the jet of water with one hand, I put the other one to use, sliding towards her and slipping my thumb inside her warm, soft pussy and pressing against her anus with my index finger.

Alma was breathing deeply, her nostrils and pupils dilated, her lips slightly parted, her cheeks flushed, her nipples bright pink and erect, her heart beating fast, her labia and clitoris swollen.

I pushed my finger slowly up her bottom, my index and thumb pressing towards each other within her velvety yet tautening insides.

I pushed the index finger as deep as it would go and as she squirmed, her breathing ragged and harsh,

Alma came with a deep, long moan, her cunt and anus contracting powerfully against my thumb and finger.

Wearily we got out of the bathtub, dried each other off and, exhausted, we moved back to the bedroom and fell asleep on the kingsized bed.

A male voice, speaking in Spanish, woke us up.

'*Hola Rafael*,' said Alma, yawning. 'Give us a second. Becky won't want you to see her in bed.'

I was naked – and doing my best to disappear under the duvet.

He walked out. Alma put on a pair of black, silky pyjamas, and I put on the clothes I'd arrived in – a pair of cords, a white vest and a little cardigan.

'Will you be in trouble?' I asked.

'He won't suspect a thing,' said Alma, with a wink. 'Never does.'

We met him in the living room. I was still a little limp.

'Are you all right, Becky?' said Rafael, Alma's boyfriend, in a strong Spanish accent. 'You came back so early. It's only midnight.'

'I twisted my ankle,' I said. 'I was glad to come back, really. You know what I'm like. Always shy at parties.'

'I know,' said Rafael, smiling kindly at me.

'Yeah, and I cannot stand the small talk,' said Alma.

'We had a night in and went to bed early. Much more fun. I think we should do it again soon.'

IF ONLY FOR TONIGHT

I can't tell you anything about him as a person from that first night. Nothing about his private life, whether he worked two jobs, whether he had a passion, a love, whether he cared about the future of the Euro, whether he believed in a god, whether he felt he had lived a good life, nothing. There is nothing of note that I could add to a description of him beyond the physical. I can tell you that he was charming, that he seemed to know exactly how to treat me, that he was firm without being pushy and that he made me nervous and comfortable all at the same time. I can make those judgements solely based on a series of sensory impressions. The way he propelled me across the room with a well placed hand in the dip of my back; the way he stood up when I returned from the bathroom, the way he never laughed when I tried to be funny, but instead let a small smile spread across his face, allowing his eyes to sparkle.

Perhaps I'm making all this up. My father, the doctor, used to say that people only see what they want to see. Maybe he didn't laugh out loud, because he didn't think I was funny. Maybe none of it was genuine. But that's what I saw.

However, I am embarrassed to say that the reason I learnt so little from him is because I never really asked. I got so sidetracked by the questions he asked me, I missed any opportunity to find out about him. In my defense I do not usually talk in depth about myself; in fact this was the first time that this had happened in many years, which is why I believe I ended up saying so *much*.

Once he got me talking about myself, the flood gates were opened and out it all came. And the other reason I kept going, I think, is because I actually believed he was listening to me. Behind the coal of his eyes was the significant glint of understanding, and the more I spoke the more he seemed to absorb my pain, hide it in his bloodstream and seal it in his veins. And he looked at me. At my face. Not my breasts. Not that my breasts are really what they once were. Thinking on it, I haven't had men look at my breasts for a while now. I'm surprised I have grown accustomed to the absence of the gaze. I suppose it's all subconscious anyway. But something had been closed inside me that's for sure. Been hidden away for a long time. And this date was my... coming out party.

He had met me at the bar, picked me right out of the crowd. Must have been my slightly nervous demeanor that tipped him off. That and the fact that I was ten years older than any of the teenagers in there. (I'm becoming less and less good at working out ages. Everyone younger than me looks like a teenager. And the way they dress...). I wore my usual long black skirt and long sleeve top combo. But I wore the one with the small slash across the front. Didn't want him to think I was a complete prude.

He put his hand on the small of my back and I flinched and turned. He smiled down at me from his six foot something height. He was handsome, in an obvious way, broad-shouldered, dark, but he had a nice scar that dipped from his right cheek on to his neck and offset any obviousness in his beauty. (Why didn't I ask him about the scar? Such an obvious conversation point...)

Within a minute he had talked me into eating dinner there. He ordered the wine and recommended the specials and then he asked me what had brought me here. And I remember knowing instinctively that the question was so much more loaded than what had brought me to Islington. So I answered it. Began my sad story. I hadn't told it for a while. Not since it happened. I think betrayal and humiliation are fun for your friends to listen to at first, but after the third day of drama, it becomes boring and they look for something else to do. I haven't spent much time with them recently anyway.

But he listened to it all, and before I knew what had happened, we were already on coffee. I felt sated. Better. I had exhausted my story. I didn't need to hear it again. It was done. That was enough for me. That he'd helped me do that. That really was enough. While we settled up the bill, (he insisted, I insisted, we ended up splitting it) I decided I wanted to kiss him. No. I wanted him to kiss me. That was all. I wanted to feel him hold me tight in towards his body while his mouth slid gently up and over mine. That would be enough. Then I would go home. A kiss would signify a complete success. As we stepped outside I realized that perhaps I was expecting too much. How much of the evening had been flirtatious? Very little. I'd poured my heart out *at* him. I'd asked practically nothing of his situation. I hadn't really let him touch me. Not even invited a gentle hand on the forearm. Perhaps one slash across the front of your top isn't enough to show a decent man like this a signal? Maybe I shouldn't have been so open? Left him with no sense of mystery?

The glare of the dirty orange streetlamps signalled the end of our time together. As I glanced around for cabs, I turned my back on him, so that he could look at me unchecked. That seemed like a smart thing to do. And I guess it was because a lot sooner than I thought he would, he grabbed my arm and span me towards him. And as the air slipped past me, I tried to relax, waiting for his lips to press against mine. But they didn't. He stopped me in front of him. Kept me at arm's length, my shoulders held firmly between both his hands.

He stared at my face, his eyes flicking over its surface, like a parent looking for guilt in a child. I looked back at him, watching his eyes take stock of me. His eyebrows twisted into his forehead, as if they were whispering, sharing a confidence. I stood up to his gaze, faced it, dared it. And then slowly, oh so slowly, he brought his lips close to me. They came towards my mouth, close enough that I could feel his cool breath on my cheek. I closed my eyes and waited to melt.

After a pause, his lips finally landed on my earlobe. They kissed it softly, then pulled away again. His fingers were cupping my face. I inhaled softly, feeling the sting of the cold London air through my nostrils. It had been a while since I had felt human contact, gentle contact anyway, not the bustling and nudging that comes from living in a crowded city, but genuine, warm, *intended* contact. I realized I had missed it. He moved in again towards my ear, but, this time, his lips sidestepped it and kissed the soft bowl beneath, pressing gently down across my neck. A tingle swept my body and I felt relaxed and nervous all at once. Relaxed because I was finally getting what I didn't realize I wanted and nervous because it had been so long since I had had anything close to resembling that. I closed my eyes, indulging the moment.

He kissed all the way around the base of my neck, rotating my head in his hands, making way for his soft, stubble-flecked mouth. When he reached the base of my throat, I felt the pressure of his tongue against it and let out an involuntary little gasp. He pulled away, as if he might have done something wrong. He hadn't. I smiled at him, my teeth tugging on my bottom lip. He released his hands from my cheeks.

'I'd like to come home with you. Would you like that?'

I guess it was the first thing he'd said all night that bothered me. Not because of the sentiment, I was pleased with the sentiment, but because I wished that he had just hailed a cab and taken me home, no questions asked. I don't want to sound ungrateful, but you asked for the truth and this is all of it. No man is perfect.

I squeezed his hand. I wanted his kiss; that was all.
I had made a deal with myself. No more than a kiss. I
barely knew this man. And just because I liked his eyes,
the glint of green buried in the brown, was no reason
to change my mind now. I pulled him in towards me,
his face so close, that I could feel the molecules of air
that separated his lips from mine. I felt them dance. He
held his position for a moment. Then, behind me, he
raised his arm. A cab pulled up, and with his other arm
he opened the door for me.

'Come on,' he said, and I felt my insides smile and
the tension build. If I had to wait til we got to mine to
feel the soft hardness (as I imagined it) of his kiss, then
so be it.

The taxi driver kept clearing his throat. He man-
fully focused on the road while we sat in the back,
pretending to look out of our respective windows. I
found myself running my right hand through my hair
while the man next to me ran his fingers up and down
my leg like a jazz pianist, tickling all the right notes
that were making me shiver. I flicked my eyes to the
rear view mirror. What was the driver thinking? Could
he see that something was happening in his back seat?
Did it happen every night for him? Men and women
surreptitiously molesting each other in his peripheral
vision? He had probably seen much worse than this.
The man was only touching my leg. But there was

something about the skill with which he handled my flesh. The way it sang underneath him. The closer we got to my home, the more I began to shake like a nervous teenager. I hadn't ever moved this fast with anyone and yet now, all those books I had read seemed to make no sense. The Rules? What rules? Why wait on a night like tonight? Why play games when things were easier not to?

Because you don't know this man, I told myself. Because you've known him for one night. And you may want to see him again.

I let us linger outside my door for a moment, let his hands explore the curve of my bottom through my skirt. I thought about Mrs. China across the street. I hoped she was watching. Putting her kids to bed and glancing out the window, wondering how lonely old me had managed to bring home a tall, dark man who couldn't keep his large hands to himself. Let her talk, I thought. Let her go to bed with her alcoholic husband and wonder what had happened to her life.

I slipped the key into the door and said the obligatory, 'Excuse the mess.' There was none, and not because I had expected him to come home with me, far from it, but because I am a tidy person and I take pride in keeping my house in a better state than my life. My father believed a house reflected the person. I was always trying to cheat that tenet by maintaining a spotless home. I paused in the doorway. What kind of woman brings home a man the first night she meets him? A woman with a house like this?

As he pushed the door behind us, I felt his hand press against my waist and guide me towards the stairs as if he knew his way around better than I did. I glanced back at him and asked, 'Don't you want a drink or somethi-' but I was interrupted by his finger on my lips. 'Shhhhh,' he whispered, his eyes burrowing into my skin. And then his finger continued its journey, entering past my lips and trailing along the groove in my tongue. He kept his eyes fixed as his finger began to circle inside my mouth and my mouth unconsciously started to dance back.

As my lips caressed his finger and my teeth scraped his skin, I realized now was the time to stop this, now was the moment to be reasonable before things got out of hand. If I didn't say anything right now, right in this moment with his fingers invading my mouth, I would not be able to stop things later. Here, in the hallway, was already far enough. But before I could stop him, he released his finger and roughly turned me around back towards the stairs.

Without thinking, as if it were natural, I started to make my way up. His stare followed my bottom, and then his hands groped towards it and then grabbed my hips instead. But this time the fingers were tighter and before I could question it, my feet were no longer touching the floor. Effortlessly, he twisted me over like a mannequin, and laid me to rest, my back against the carpet of the landing, my legs dangling over the top three stairs.

The lights were off upstairs and for a moment I was glad. I didn't want to feel him watching me anymore. In fact that's not true. I wanted to feel him watching me, I just didn't want him to see me looking back. I couldn't let him know that I didn't want him to stop, even though my voice kept threatening to say it, something kept repressing it.

I lay my head back, not wanting to see what he might do, just trying to let it happen. Whatever this man chose to do with me, I had no choices left. I lost that luxury when he had his hand in my mouth.

He made himself comfortable on the stairs, tracing a finger up and down my legs, admiring them as a blind man might. And then his mouth began to work its way along my stockings (thank god I was wearing stockings!), pressing his tongue along the fabric, hard in places so I could feel it on my skin. I held my breath. He kept coming closer to my pussy, but whenever I could feel him edging towards it, he would edge back again. He began to kiss my ankles, seeming to savour them as he reached up and let his nimble fingers roll down each stocking until they were silk doughnuts at my feet.

I squeezed my eyes tight, not to let him in, not to allow him to see the spirals that might be spinning inside my pupils. He lifted my waist, again, lifted it like it weighed nothing, and deftly removed my panties in a style that, had I been thinking hard at the time, would have suggested he had done this before. And then he was kissing my inner thigh, kissing it hard, working on it, like it was something he would eat when it was tender enough.

Then nothing.

I opened my eyes and blinked up at the dark ceiling. The sound of his breathing corrupted the silence. I wondered if I should speak. Wondered if I should move. Was he expecting me to do something now? Was I wrong to be just lying here? What was he doing?

And then I felt it. His mouth just above the edge of my pussy. His tongue right on the precipice, frozen, as if preparing to leap. But still nothing moved as if his whole body had turned to stone. The only sign of life was his breath which fell in slow hot waves against my pubic bone, sending spasms through my spine. My pussy began a dialogue with his mouth, begging his tongue to make contact, pleading with it, and as my wetness began to blot out on the carpet beneath me, I swear I could hear it screaming.

But still he waited.

His tongue remained poised, silent, torturing me. And while it waited, his hand reached up to my bra. Four bands of flesh pulsated between his fingers as he squeezed my breast. I was just about to cry out, to tell him to end it, to do *something*, that he was making me angry, when, with no warning, with no sense of decorum, his tongue dove inside me. There was a sharp stabbing in my stomach, but an ecstatic stabbing, a stabbing like my blood had been blocked in my veins and now it was flowing freely. My body lurched forward, and my hands involuntarily gripped his hair as if I might fall over if I didn't hold on to something, anything, even though I was, in actuality, lying down. The way his tongue worked inside me, the way it made figures of eight around my clitoris, the way it made figures of *art* inside me, lapping in and out and around was like nothing I had ever experienced. At the same time, his hands worked my breasts, at once gently teasing my nipples, then squeezing the whole breast, then stroking them softly, then forcing them together, then keeping them apart. For a second, he squeezed too hard, making me flinch, but before I could complain, the pain was replaced by soft treatment, and the soft treatment made me miss the pain and he seemed to read that and then squeeze again and I found my hands helping his, entwining in his fingers, pressing them harder into my own flesh.

It was like the listening, it was like *everything* this man had done tonight, it was *not what I was used to*. The men I'd experienced before had been, at best, dutiful, their bi-quarterly dips into cunnilingus, functional and grudging and it had taken strength from me to come, because although it felt good, there was always the nagging feeling in the back of my mind that they weren't happy down there, that it might not taste right, that the smell might be too much. But he, *this man*, he *loved my pussy*. There was no other way to describe it. No one could fake the way his tongue behaved around it. If his tongue had had a mouth of its own, it would have devoured it.

My bottom was digging rhythmically into the floor, harder and harder, and I could feel the spikes of the carpet dappling my skin in red patches. My ribs pitched and fell as I tried to weather the oncoming storm of orgasms. It was too soon, it was ridiculous, I didn't even know him and yet, here he was, not teasing, but *tearing* orgasms out of me, one after the other, I was screaming, I was lost, tufts of his hair were coming out in my hands and yet he kept on going, kept on pushing and pushing with his mouth, his lips enveloping the opening to myself, his tongue working within the seal, exploring for anything it may have missed, and all my pussy could cry was *please no more*

I can't breathe you're killing me you have to stop, don't stop, stop, but if you do stop I might die and if I die I know I'll miss you...

And then all at once, I pushed his head away and rolled over. I curled up, foetally, my hands folded between my legs, holding myself, trying to catch my breath, trying to regain some sensation of the real world. It wasn't right to feel this lost, lying here, on my landing, losing myself in the darkness of the night, away from Mrs. China, away from work, away from all the let downs, the when-will-my-life-begins, the ever-dwindling supply of my potential... How could this be so... dramatically, so wonderfully... *removed*? And could it ever last beyond this moment?

He crawled dutifully up the stairs and lay down behind me. He was out of breath. He fitted his arm snugly across my midriff, his face in my hair, breathing in my smell. I didn't know until he held me like that that I was crying. Crying because I'd let it go this far, crying because I hadn't been touched like this in three years, crying because it had never been like this, crying because I had *missed* it, and crying because this is how I'd let it happen.

I let him hold me for a half an hour. He didn't say a word. I smiled to myself. Maybe he was perfect. I cleared my throat. Prepared myself.

'Can I...' I paused, terrified of the answer. 'Will

I... be able to see you again? Or was this just... a one-off?' He leant forward on an elbow, stroking my face. I stared at the wall, scared to meet his eyes. 'Of course you can.' I saw the clock on the wall. 'Next time, just ask for me by name.'

He leant down and kissed me on the cheek. 'I'd better go. Thank you. I had a wonderful evening.'

And as he was about to make his way out the door, treading carefully down the stairs, as if I lived with anyone who might wake up, I got to my feet, naked from the waist down and ran to him. His hand was on the latch and this time I held *his* face in my hands.

'Will you kiss me on the mouth next time?'

He looked down at me from his six foot four frame. I tried to ignore the uncomfortable flash of pity that crossed over his eyes.

'Let's not spoil this.'

He turned back and kissed my neck again, one final imprint.

'You're wonderful,' he said.

And as his taxi pulled away I glanced out the window and hoped that Mrs. China hadn't spotted another man leaving me crying at the door.

STUDIED

When Natasha circled the small ad in the *Spectator* she hadn't really intended to respond. But that was when she was still in denial about John. Since she had heard that John had become engaged to his ex, Sara, it had begun to dawn on Natasha that she had only ever been a pawn in their game – even if the bastard *had* lived with her for the last year. Now, after two glasses of a robust Chianti consumed alone in her Queen's Park flat, the curious offer contained in the ad began to seem to Natasha like salvation.

Italian artist requires life model. You must sit still for me for one week in my Tuscan villa and I will provide all your needs. Please send photo.

Secrets

The awkward use of English had first amused
Natasha, but now it intrigued her. Was the artist a man
or a woman? How old was he or she… and had they
intended the ambiguity in that phrase about her needs?
Natasha took a sip of wine and as the sultry taste of
Tuscany undressed her taste buds she came to an
uncharacteristically reckless decision. Moments later
she found herself frantically searching for an attractive
photograph of herself.

Three weeks later Natasha received a package
containing an airline ticket and a handwritten letter in
charming English inviting her to Villa Carla in Tuscany.
It was signed 'Claudio.' Her doubts soon gave way to
curiosity and in the days before the journey Natasha
had allowed herself to imagine, hope even, that the
artist would be young, beautiful, and unmarried.

By the day of the flight Claudio had become a
mellifluously titled and rather taller version of
Leonardo di Caprio with a long dark mane. As she
walked into the small arrivals hall in Pisa, it occurred
to Natasha that whoever was there to meet her was
likely to be a disappointment. Even this thought,
however, did not prevent the sinking sensation she felt
when she saw the grey-haired man holding the sign
that boasted 'Villa Carla.'

Claudio, she discovered as he drove her around the
beautiful walled city of Lucca, was a widower in his

sixties. But her disappointment quickly faded as it became clear that her host was witty, charming and good looking in a patrician sort of way. Natasha imagined that he must once have been a master of seduction, and she soon relaxed at the thought that although she wouldn't be having wild sex with him, she could certainly enjoy a week of flattering flirting.

On their arrival Claudio showed Natasha to her room and left her to unpack. From her window she could see the olive terraces dropping away down the hillside beneath her and there, standing amongst them, a beautiful young man. What a pity it is not he who is the artist, she sighed to herself. She watched the young man spreading a net underneath an olive tree, then pause. She caught her breath and felt a thrill pass through her as she observed him languidly with-draw his penis and begin to masturbate. By the time he brought himself to orgasm she, too, was touching herself. Natasha was nearing her own release when she was interrupted by a knock at the door. It was Claudio summoning her to the studio where he wished to begin work immediately.

As he led her through a pergola and up a gentle incline to his studio in a converted outbuilding, Claudio patiently explained his vision. The subject for his painting was to be 'The reluctant bride' and in his symbolic representation a beautiful young woman is to be seen reclining and wearing nothing but a blindfold. Natasha had expected and prepared herself to pose nude and as Claudio prepared his materials, she undressed behind a screen and slipped on a silk robe hanging there. As she crossed the room and took up her position on a revolving dais, Natasha felt a frisson of vulnerability as she let the robe fall and stood before him. Claudio spoke softly as he stepped forward to arrange her position and gently secure the blindfold.

Natasha sat patiently as Claudio worked. Slowly relaxing into the silence her thoughts wandered and she didn't notice the small click of the studio door opening and closing. Occasionally the artist approached her to re-arrange her slightly – lift her chin or shift her leg. His touch was confident, strong, and gentle – his smell warm and sweet, too. Sometimes she could sense his presence near her without him touching her. For a woman accustomed to control, Natasha was surprised to discover that she was beginning to enjoy herself. Against her conscious wishes she noticed the stirrings of desire and was surprised to find herself wanting to be touched again by the old man she could not see.

Nothing more than a cough and the closing of the studio door signalled the end of the session and when she finally removed the blindfold Natasha found herself alone in the studio with the painting. Still naked she ventured across to the easel and was pleasantly surprised to discover that the painting, although still in its early stages, was clearly going to be very good.

Natasha was surprised by the sudden re-entry of Claudio into the room. He laughed as she stole behind the screen and clumsily reached for her clothes – why this sudden modesty after all that professional intimacy? As she dressed he turned away to cover the picture and put away his paints and Natasha was suddenly aware that she felt differently in his presence now. With the blindfold removed, her reserve had returned and her desire had cooled.

Joining Claudio for dinner later, Natasha was surprised when the youth she had seen tossing himself off in the olive grove that morning entered with steaming bowls, brimming with rich farro soup. As he approached her and silently served her she was puzzled by a sense of more than visual familiarity. Observing her tension, Claudio smiled and introduced Giorgio as his son. When she turned to smile at him the youth shrunk back slightly and Claudio laughed again as he explained that although he understands English, sadly Giorgio is unable to speak it.

Claudio watched as her eyes followed Giorgio from the room and as the door closed behind him he explained further, 'My son does not speak English. In fact he doesn't speak at all, not since he was born.

Naturally this makes him shy.' Later, emboldened by the rich Brunello she was drinking, Natasha returned to the subject of his son and began to encourage Claudio to let Giorgio go free, to make his way in the world. She was already beginning to form ideas of bringing him to England. Again, she soon found Claudio's easy manner and warmth disarmingly charming. 'I am an old artist and now I am happy just to have you here, to look... no, I should better say admire. But he needs more of course, not only me. I think maybe you understand. You saw him amongst the olive trees, no?' Natasha wondered if Claudio had noticed her flush.

Natasha slept well that night and dreamed of Giorgio silently bearing her on horseback across gently undulating Tuscan hills – one arm wrapped around his strong midriff and the other clasping his swollen cock.

The following day, nude and blindfolded once more, Natasha resumed her place and position in the studio. Silence fell as Claudio began to work and Natasha allowed herself to return to that waking dream with Giorgio lifting her down and laying her on a bank. As he gently parted her legs with his knee and lowered himself onto her and then slowly into her, she was brought back to the studio by the sound of a door opening and shutting. And now, in the silence, Natasha became keenly aware of the artist's presence near her – his familiar scent, the sound of his movements and the rhythmic undulations of his breathing. Her excitement turned suddenly to panic as she became convinced that Claudio could read her thoughts and she felt the hairs on her arms rise, her skin tingle and a wetness coming below.

For the first time she broke the silence: 'Claudio?' Hearing no reply Natasha wondered whether she was alone and, as her senses searched the silence, she found herself fighting back an urgent desire to touch herself. Then, with a stabbing shock, came his touch and wave that throbbed through her body. She thrilled at his lightness and suddenly became acutely aware of her nipples stiffening. Natasha was in a state of silent confusion, of fear and ecstasy. Now an idea was beginning to form in her mind and now it was not just her instincts that she decided to follow, but also her suspicions. Without his bidding she moved her thighs slightly apart and breathed in his smell as she felt her pussy moisten further and the man close in. She was more than ready when she felt his strong hand push up the inside of her thigh towards her entrance.

'It's you, isn't it, Giorgio?' she whispered. The hand hesitated in its gradual progress and silence filled the room. Then, softly and slowly, the fingers returned to their quest for her softness. Natasha was sure of it now and parted her legs further. She couldn't help but let out a sudden gasp as she felt the man's lips caress her nipple, and as his head moved down she could feel Giorgio's curly hair gently stroking her stomach. Abandoning herself now, she felt a delirious sense of relief and pleasure as she lost her fingers in his curls and pushed his head down further.

With her hips lifted and thighs wrapped around the man's head, Natasha's breathing was becoming shorter and with shocking haste she felt herself shudder involuntarily as waves of pleasure overtook her. She offered no resistance as she felt the man's hands on her hips lifting her and turning her. On all fours now she felt his stiff prick pushing into her from behind and her wetness envelope him. As Giorgio's beautiful cock grew wider and harder within her, and his thrusts became fiercer and deeper, she felt herself rising to meet his imminent explosion with another of her own.

Still blindfolded, she moaned aloud as Giorgio's strong hands clasped her buttocks as he pulled her up to meet him and she felt his balls thud against her arse as his he sank his cock deep within her. In the euphoria of her ecstasy it was several seconds before she became aware of another pair of hands now untying her blind fold. When the silk sash was finally withdrawn from her face with a flourish, she was both shocked and thrilled to see Claudio sitting before her, wearing a broad smile. 'Why would I ever want him to leave?' he shrugged, as he sat before her massaging his own erection. Lost in waves of pleasure, she watched him watching her as she and his son climaxed together, and in the moment of her release Natasha smiled as a thought crossed her mind – this was one game she was more than happy to be a pawn in.

A TASTE OF HONEY

Email to Emma from the MD of Creative Cuisine Agency, January 6th

Hi Emma. Can we book you to cater for the Writers' Study Group again? It begins next week for a fortnight. They're based at the Calvingham Studios. This year they are splitting the course into three and spreading it throughout the year. They've somehow managed to get the *famed* New York writer Gabriel Findlay to lead the whole course. He is surely going to be bored stiff by all of those try-hard attendees! By the way, he is also famed for his good looks – phwoar! Enjoy. Must say I am jealous. It's the usual; you prepare dinner for twenty on the Friday/Saturday/ Sunday nights and they self cater for the rest. You won't need to hang around. They don't need too much of your literary hostess act (as good as it is), they are bound to only have eyes for Gabriel (male and female alike). Take it easy for a change. Much love, Jane x

(P.S. Can you invoice at the end of each job? If we keep the contract that means 3 weeks in January, 3 in April and 3 weeks later in July.)

Emma's journal, Friday Jan 12th
Busy day. Mostly 'work work work'. In bed 11pm. Should be in town living it up but am too tired… as always. God, am sick of moaning to this diary. When will something happen?

(Not much to note about the 'famed writer'. Not *that* good looking – though I do like his quiet, monumental air. Bound to be a complete bastard and neurotic.) Luckily the minions were on top form so handed over to them as soon as I had carved the beef. Was out of there before pudding.

Tomorrow I will plant out my garden. The fruits and flowers have arrived from the nursery.

Emma's journal, Saturday Jan 13th
… back late. Dinner went well. All writers replete and smiley and full of praise… except Gabriel. He just stares and thinks, as if only tuned to his own inner monologue. Disconcerting. Interesting. A little thrilling. He is *quite* good looking, I suppose.

Secrets

Email from Gabriel to Emma, Tuesday Jan 16th
Dear Emma. Sorry to disturb you midweek. We are looking forward to your delicious food again this weekend. In fact we are all a little bit bored with having to cope on our own during the week. I am also sick of the students, hence me bribing the agency for your email (forgive me?). Permit me to buy you dinner tomorrow evening… if only to save me from another lonely take-away? Yours, Gabriel.

Emma's journal, Wednesday Jan 17th
After much debate accepted GF's invitation. Both of us behaved in very decorous fashion. Sigh. Much talk of books, film, art. He does have good taste, I will give him that. And those eyes! I felt pierced. He is attractive. Actually.

Email from Gabriel to Emma, Monday Jan 22nd
You did it again this weekend. We can't live without you. The theme of feasting has even entered the students' valiant scribbles. Have begun to think that Friday–Sunday are the only days of the week (the rest I call 'nights'). I imagine that you are now lost somewhere in your garden. It's only Monday morning (I have nipped to the office while the scribblers take a break from the monotony of me). Can't bear the thought of dining alone. Come with me? Your beloved Chinatown?

A Taste of Honey

Email from Emma to Gabriel, Tuesday Jan 23rd
G.— Thanks v. much. Had lovely time. By the way you are wrong about Chinese film. The underpinning symbolism in *Red Sorghum* is about sex as ownership; *Raise the Red Lantern* is about sex as power. I prefer the latter (film). E x

Email Gabriel to Emma, Wednesday Jan 24th
Take me to dinner or lose me forever. Seriously. I might slip into an anorexic stupor. I hate eating alone and I cannot be with the scribblers 24/7. x

Emma's journal, Wednesday Jan 24th
… quick entry as it is very late (and am bit tipsy). Dinner on Monday *and* Wednesday is all a bit much. He is beguiling. And those eyes. But he has a wife! And she has a name! Frances. Poor Frances! Actually, how about poor me? He hasn't done anything that Frances could worry about… poor *me*. No! It's wrong. Am very cross. Actually am a little disappointed — he is gorgeous. And smells intoxicatingly of cedar… Anyway he leaves on Saturday night — thank goodness.

Lily of the Valley coming through in the garden.

Emma's journal, Saturday Jan 27th
Am confused. After two weeks of alabaster charm and decorum (but *attentive* decorum) he hardly speaks to

me at the end-of-course party. Surrounded by the adoration of the scribblers I know but... he hardly came near me. I had been hoping that we would at least finish one of our babbles about the anguish of metaphysical poets or the beauty of Chinese art-house film... but, absolutely *nothing*. Afterward,s we all lurched rather tipsily towards an unknown club in the tow of one of the younger (and definitely more flirty) scribblarians, her cleavage shining as a beacon, to the three or four ageing male writers in the pack, in the gloom of the Soho night. I was secretly smarting with jealousy and miscomprehension, only tagging along with the writing students because it meant I was still near to Gabriel. Pathetic. I blame the champagne. I blame myself. I blame my obsessive crush on that tall, impassive, hypocritical, hypnotising, two-timing, completely captivating and plainly beautiful man.

I was all ready to slip away from the tottering troupe towards the No.19 bus when a miracle occurred: suddenly I felt a guiding hand at my elbow, directing me firmly and quite decidedly towards a blackened shop front. I thought at first that it was a sex shop but once inside the deep shadows of the vestibule Gabriel was welcomed as an old friend by the exquisitely dressed girl at the reception. She welcomed us into a room that refused to reveal itself fully because it was so dimly lit by lamps on the two rows of little tables. I walked ahead of Gabriel's guiding hand, feeling an electrical pulse in the small of my back, even though he did not touch me. I resonated. The waiter offered a central table but Gabriel motioned towards a small round table and crimson velvet banquet in the corner. We slipped in and sat down. Gabriel pressed in behind me (too close?) and ordered red wine. He told me that he had been longing to come to this place since he had heard it recommended by one of the more clubbable dandies on the course. The dandy, it transpired had agreed to secure him a table. (Had this been planned? Would he have come alone?)

We sat in easy silence. We breathed the same rhythm. I drank it all in. The crimson corner. The pillow of his lip. As he talked I watched his mouth, thinking 'let him kiss me with the kisses of his mouth'. Would he kiss me? My god I hoped so. What is it in the *Song of Solomon*? 'Thy lips are like a thread of scarlet'? His are like a bed of scarlet — I want to lie next to him with my lips just brushing his. And breathe cedar.

As he talked, and when I laughed, or when I dared to be penetrated by his gaze, I could have sworn that he would touch me. I cannot promise. But I'm sure, I think. The tip of his finger would alight on the naked inner slope of my forearm, the side of his calf would rest against mine, gently pressing home a shared understanding. It feels now as if he was planting himself under my skin.

I was, I am, hooked: my flesh sewn into his at each and every point of coincidence.

Suddenly, I was in the sharp, cold air, on the trail of his poor flock, now knee deep in drunken revelry in a shambolic jazz joint. I felt pulled out of the womb too soon. We descended to their level. The scribblarians were all pissed now, and pawing, especially the small be-cleavaged one. But he stood his ground. And he stood by me. And I was intoxicated by his proximity and made immobile. And my body still resonated. And I breathed but lightly so as not to dispel the dream. Then, agonizingly, slowly, little by little, he moved away, falling deeper and deeper into the warm body of his apostles.

And now I am home without his beloved prose woven through my body.

Handwritten note in bunch of flowers of Lily of the Valley and white hyacinths left on Emma's doorstep: Sunday Jan 28th
E – thanks for everything. I am glad that I missed my plane; I couldn't have passed those hours so happily without your company. P.S. Lily of the Valley symbolise the return of happiness – I know you love your hidden meanings. G x

A Taste of Honey

Emma's journal, Sunday Jan 28th
And then the flowers turn up. Of course he missed his plane! He was due to fly on Saturday wasn't he? Did he do it on purpose? Did he stay for me? But then… the hyacinths? They symbolise a game – I looked it up.

What was he playing at?

At least he left before he got his pudding.

~

Email from Gabriel to Emma, April 7th
Emma, hello. How are you? How is your garden? See, I do listen. I imagine you sitting among your lilies. Chose *Raise the Red Lantern* when Frances suggested a DVD night. It has a strange recurring thing of denied passion – ironic that I saw it with Frances. Frances does not like music, nor film – nor, I believe, does she like art.

Email from Emma to Gabriel, April 7th
Does she like you?

Email from Gabriel to Emma, April 10th
As much as you do?

Email from Emma to Gabriel, April 10th
What exactly do you mean?

Email from Gabriel to Emma, April 10th
Emma - I would like to hold you. Frances does not like
being held.

Email from Gabriel to Emma, April 12th
Scratch that. I was drunk – sorry.

Emma's journal, April 13th
Gabriel. Gabriel. Gabriel.
Lilies not out of course. Too cold yet.

*Card from Gabriel to Emma (picture of Empire State
Building), postmarked April 13th*
E. It seems increasingly chilly in NYC. GF x

*Emailed memo from Emma to Jane of The Creative Cuisine
Agency, April 14th:*
Hi Jane – sorry, all minions busy for second writers'
dinner contract. Will do myself. Good to keep my
hand in. Love Emma x

*Email from Gabriel to Emma [with attachment of the verses
of the* Song of Solomon*], April 15th*
Dear Emma – the second course is upon us. Am looking
forward to your feasts – if not to the eager scribblers.

I have found these verses from the *Song of Solomon*
while preparing a paper for the poor dears on the

theme of food – you see you have me at it now. You would love them, it's full of food and garden references. I am almost hypnotised by their erotic tension. Who can read *Thy lips, O my spouse, drop as the honeycomb: honey and milk are under thy tongue...* and remain sane?

If nothing else, I thought you might like to deepen your days with crimson thought – at least it won't be lost on you and my efforts will not be for nought. May it lubricate the parts of your mind needed to honey the willing students with your post-prandial banter – they do love you (and your food). *Because of the savour of thy good ointments thy name is as ointment poured forth.*

Is it literature or the correspondent who is my mistress here?

Would love to tell Frances that we discuss lust and power (in the name of literature of course), but I fear she wouldn't care. She doesn't like poetry anyway – or rather she prefers art, or whatever that stuff in her gallery down town can be called.

Looking forward to seeing you when I come to London again. Tomorrow? GF

Emma's journal, April 15th
Can hardly breath. Feel skewered by coincidence. Can he read my mind? Screw meaning.

Is he an assassin?

Emma's journal, April 16th

Nothing! Just more words! He arrives from NYC, takes me out for dinner and makes no move! Does he just want me for my food? My garden? No more talking. I know my *Song* now off by heart, and I repeat it throughout the day like a demented mantra. I want him *to lie all night betwixt my breasts*. God please let me lay my lips against his thread of scarlet. I want his left hand under my head and his right hand to embrace me. In fact I want it to sway slowly back and forth over my tightening belly, to move up my centre line and trace fire around my breasts. I want to hold my breath and arch my back and press my belly and hips into the marble tower that is his body. I want to replace his words, which sink deep into me, with kisses. I want his mouth, his body, his whole being, to redefine itself between my legs and infiltrate me. I want him to pierce my quivering carapace, and penetrate my soul.

Oh Gabriel! Reach inside me; pull me inside out. Sing up through me. Perfect each sinew of my body until they vibrate in unison and a silent scream marks surrender...

By night on my bed I sought him whom my soul loveth: I sought him, but I found him not.

Email from Emma to Gabriel, April 17th

Dear G. I prefer the metaphysical poets, normally. You

know, *To his Coy Mistress* et al. To me the chase is the thing, at least for a while. But games can pall Gabriel. Two days ago I felt rescued by your *Song of Solomon*. But now I think that you have simply hooked me with it. Honest literary sex talk is a hallowed thing for a single girl like me and those passages seem (almost) capable of resuscitating body and soul. I imagine my voice in the *Song* passages. I read them over and over again. It's intoxicating and not a little obsessive. I wish I could replicate it all in my garden – mandrake I can grow, but pomegranates?! E

Gabriel's diary, April 29th
Last day teaching. Call Frances (not ticked). Confirm flights!! Emma drink?

Scribbled note in Gabriel's diary over appoinments for April 30th
Why did I not take her?

Letter from Gabriel to Emma (not sent), April 30th
Emma. I would have fucked you; shot stars into your broadening galaxies. I want to. I want to pin you to the sheets, and plunder you... to hoist you on my mast, to plunge, raid and rage inside you. Moisten you. Penetrate you. Fill you...almost cleave you. Corrupt, contain and create you.

I want to make you express animal sounds unheard before; I want to entreat you to sigh; I want to cajole filth from you and perhaps command some screaming…

But you deserve better.

❧

Email from Emma to Gabriel, June 1st
G, I imagine that I am embarrassing myself now as I have not heard from you after five emails. I will stop. E

Emma's journal, June 15th
Today I sat amid the lilies of my garden. And tried not to think of the *Song*.

Note in bunch of tuberoses delivered to Emma, July 14th
Sorry not to have been in touch – I will be in London from 15th (your birthday?) at the Mantle Hotel in Marylebone.

Postcard to Gabriel left at the reception of the Mantle Hotel, July 16th
Last night was beautiful. You are a gardener to my garden. It cannot happen again. Your choice of tuberoses said it all: it's too dangerous – you have Frances, and I have my sanity (just).

Hand-written note to Emma delivered in a box of chocolates, July 16th
Another performance?
Arrive at 10pm wearing nothing but a smile (like the one you have now).

Emma's journal entry, July 16th
I am an idiot.

Text to Gabriel from Emma, July 16th
Read your email. Now.

Email from Emma to Gabriel, July 16th
I have bathed in a hot bath until my skin is pink and dripping with scented oil. My breasts and belly are anointed for you. I dragged a track with my index finger, imagining it was your tongue, from my pussy, slowly through my pubic hair and up, up, up, agonisingly slowly to my navel. There I paused where the glistening drops of unguent stick to my skin and breathe with shallow breaths imagining that this is the blueprint of your later moves. I now drag all four fingers of my left hand up to my right breast as I type and knead the plump promising form while my nipple hardens under the care of my palm. This is for you. This is all for you.

Secrets

Emma's journal entry, July 26th

It's nearly over. The week has passed as an orgy of the flesh. His tongue is an outrageous intruder. His hands can conduct symphonies from a keyboard of bone and strings of sinew. His cock, unsheathed, is a weapon of such penetration that when he moves in me, he moves up me and through me. His mouth shoots passages of purple prose through my soul until every muscle contracts in star-bright spasms. The ghost of this sex will haunt me, even when another possesses me, yet exorcism of this will be a sin to the flesh. And I? I feel screwed of all meaning. And I don't care. I'm quite deliciously and unrepentantly shocked at what I am capable of doing to another body.

Letter from Emma to Gabriel, postmarked July 26th

Gabriel, my angel,

This surreal, hyperreal, connection of the body is about to end. The points where you have touched me are scorched with memories. Saturday is your last night and you will be surrounded by the adoring horde after the reading performances. I will say goodbye now while I alone have your attention. Thank you.

Yours ever, Emma x

Emma's journal, July 27th
No word from Gabriel.

A Taste of Honey

*Hand-written note delivered to Emma with a box containing
a red silk corset tied with black ribbons, July 28th*
Allow the girl who delivers this to come in and dress
you. Do not put on any other garment. Come to the
reading alone. Order your minions to sort out the
canapés because you will leave before the puddings are
brought out. The *Song* will be manifest in your body.

~

Emma's journal, August 15th
I have been walking around in a daze. Everything I
touch reminds me of Gabriel. The figs in my garden
are dropping uncollected and the grapes are ripening
on the vine. The lilies drop their heavy heads as if they
are almost spent. I do not care.

I have not, until now, been able to record the events
of that night in the fear that in the effort of recall the
memories might fade away. But now I realise that as
each day puts corporeal Gabriel further from me, I
need to capture him here where he will not be lost.

I had returned from preparing the food for the end-
of-course party to get changed when a knock at the door
disturbed me in my bath. An attractive young woman
stood on the step holding exquisitely wrapped
packages. I recognised Gabriel's handwriting on the
note she handed me. As I read his instructions my

evening opened ahead of me on a wave of crimson possibilities.

She dressed me in the bedroom. I rocked back rhythmically each time she pulled and tightened the lacing of the corset until the flesh of my full breasts quivered with expectation above the boning and ribbons. She helped me slip into the sheath of silk skirt, which skimmed my hips. She buttoned the slightly translucent Victorian blouse so that a pretty amount of cleavage quivered visibly as I breathed. She left as I walked to the mirror on spiked-heeled shoes that fitted perfectly. There were no other under-garments. The remaining package contained a heady perfume of tuberose; another envelope and a small bottle marked 'Take me later'.

I read the new instructions greedily and followed them to the letter. I arrived at the venue slightly late and took my reserved seat in the front row just as Gabriel's reading had begun. He stared at me as he recited his lines and I was excited by the knowledge that he knew I was wearing no knickers. The stage lighting spilled slightly off the podium and caught my décolletage shivering for him lightly and expectantly. I heard Gabriel speak but I did not hear the words. I just looked at his eyes, at his mouth, at his thighs, his strong hands. I undressed him in my mind. And he knew it.

As the applause subsided I stood up and floated, as

if in a dream, among the scribblers and my minions rushing around with trays. The waiting seemed interminable and the little silver vial seemed to glow silently in the palm of my hand. I spoke to no one. At the allocated time I walked to the door where a taxi waited for me and I read the last note on the little bottle. 'Take me in your mouth and on your lips. I want to taste you when you arrive'. I decanted the contents nervously and tasted… honey. I was terrified that I would have to speak to the taxi driver but he just drove off the moment I sat down. I concentrated on keeping a pool of the honey under my tongue battling against the rising sweet tides in my mouth. I smiled and traced with my middle finger a glistening track of the crystalline liquid over my bottom lip.

Suddenly the taxi stopped and the man said the fare had been paid. A doorman was waiting to help me out. I stalked silently through the lobby and up to Gabriel's room.

To my surprise a young man opened the door. I stepped in. I could not see Gabriel but I knew he was there because the warm smell of cedar pervaded the air. The young man blindfolded me and led me gently to the middle of the room. I heard the door close with a click and I wondered with a start how many people were now looking at me. I said Gabriel's name but there was no answer.

And then I felt his hands. I inclined my head as they stroked my neck and the cupped mounds of my breasts. They unbuttoned my shirt, slid up between my legs, stroked my pussy. I swayed slightly on my heels but stayed silent. And still he didn't kiss me. The skirt was removed. The blouse too. And then shockingly and suddenly he cut the stays of the corset and it fell to the floor. And still he didn't kiss me. He lead me to the bed and lay me down and with his left hand under my head he traced his lines of fire with his right from my breast to my pussy… and then with an agonisingly beautiful slowness he circled my clit, drawing up a hypnotising rhythm which caused fires in my cunt and my breasts screamed for his mouth. And then… and then… and then… as the stars gathered behind my eyes he penetrated my mouth with his tongue and all was honey…

I was startled from a drowsy reverie when I heard the click of the door latch. I realised that the smell of cedar was gone.

Letter from Gabriel to Emma, August 21st
I will rise now, and go about the city in the streets. I walk about like a ghost. I live a half-life amongst buildings and words. But when I read, I am with you in your garden and, like a bee, I will always have a craving for honey.

THE FAVOURITE GAME

I looked down at my feet, encased in Charles Jourdan black 4-inch-heels, and tried to see myself as you must have seen me – walking hesitantly back and forth across my office while you feigned interest in our mortgage terms. It was the ankle straps that sealed the deal, inspiring you to comment. Your eyes had darted to them within a few seconds of our meeting. You had waited for me to follow your line of sight, so you could jump in with the leading question, somewhat breathless, a little delirious: 'Do you always wear shoes as captivatingly erotic as those?'

How I envied you that brave opening gambit, so loaded with information about your sexual proclivities, yet phrased so politely as to be flattering to me. How on earth was I to answer without resorting to predictable British denial: 'What, these? Oh, I simply had nothing else to wear!' or somesuch jocular quip that would have thrown a blanket over the potential for exploration. That would have been my typical response. Yet even in those first few moments of our meeting, I was undergoing such a profound *satori* of relief – someone had noticed something so personal about me – that I realized it was no time for modesty, false or otherwise. I wanted to tell you everything – about me, about my fetishes, about the things I did when I was alone.

'It's the straps that make them just that bit special, isn't it?' I replied. 'I like clothes with straps and belts and buckles. All my shoes are erotic in some way.' I finished off with a little unnecessary justification, waving my hand almost dismissively: 'It's my... thing.'

There. I'd done it. Played the adult answer to your very adult inquiry. I hadn't let myself down, apart from those final three words.

The office heating system made metallic noises around us as we faced each other in silent, prickly anticipation, like two scorpions in a pit. Then you launched into a conversation about property and fixed interest rates while I drifted into a reverie about how I had waited years for someone like you to ask me questions so I could admit to my secrets, my perversions. I wanted you to tease them to the surface so they remained suppressed no longer. All my guilty indulgences. All those evenings I'd spent purposely uncomfortable – hobbled in pencil skirts, lying foetal on my bed, gagged with a scarf by my own hands, my legs strapped tightly together, aching for the treatment I craved – would be secrets no more. They would belong to you. Now you had made an appointment with your new mortgage broker I could be liberated into bondage: a sweet, oxymoronic irony only the cognoscenti could appreciate.

We went through the motions of discussing your intended acquisition. I leaned in close to point out repayment terms, the mortgage protection plan, and all the little sweeteners that made our company competitive. You, meanwhile, could read the small print at your leisure; it was the curve of my back and gently flaring hips that had your attention at that moment. When we looked at each other to converse, the subtextual dialogue was so loud it was like having a third person in the room.

We kept proceedings businesslike, even though I knew your request for brochures at the other side of the office was a ruse to get me up and walking on those pretty heels, noting the tension in my calf muscles, the restriction of movement in my gait. When I handed you my card I begged the forces of

dark desire that you would return soon... and the
games could begin.

~≋~

You called five hours later, telling me you wanted
to take me to dinner that night — to a discreet Thai
restaurant in Bayswater that was conducive to intimate
conversation. I was being called upon to be braver
sooner than I had anticipated. When we met at the bar
just down the road from the restaurant, I was worried
there would be an awkwardness, those moments of
mundane reality that encroach on soon-to-be lovers —
when ordering drinks or looking for wallets is just
too perfunctory. I was spared any discomfort by your
order to find a seat and, once you were beside me, I
launched into talking about my love for Italian horror
films and industrial music. You didn't quite get my
obscure Gothic references, but you were willing to
appreciate we had been led to the same fetishistic
temple by different routes, to play complementary parts.

You were 48, well-groomed and had a fantastic
head of thick, grey hair, neatly cut but not too short.
You owned property in London and Cheshire. You ran
a design company and had clearly defined ideas about
style. Your manners were as impeccable as your suit,
and you looked more grown up than anyone I'd ever

dated. You even had one of those overcoats that daddies and diplomats carry around with them on winter nights. You dressed like a man rather than an overgrown boy and were attentive to everything I needed. When we adjourned to the restaurant I was alarmed at first when you ordered for me, but I accepted the game was underway the moment we'd sat down, and I wasn't about to make a stand for political correctness.

During the starter, I listened as you spoke about your erstwhile 'playmates' – the games of master and servant you enjoyed over the course of a weekend at your country home. I sipped eagerly at the wine, as if a little inebriation would ease the digestion of your anecdotes. I heard of women who liked to be thrashed in dungeons, who would have you dress as their doctor, their priest, or their former headmaster, and how you willingly obliged. You did your best to shock me, but I showed no alarm. You occasionally stopped to ask me if whatever you had just mentioned might be something I'd like. I nodded at everything. You were now my confessor. When I gave broad brushstrokes to my fantasies your eyes shone at the prospect of making them real. You told me the sight of a pair of inflamed buttocks at the rear end of a well-educated professional woman was the red rag to your bull of lust – the spur to action you couldn't resist. My head was soon dizzy with stars.

During dinner you told me what a lovely voice I had. You asked me if I had ever realized my needs. I recalled the sorry story of my 10-year relationship with Andy. We'd met at uni and had lived together until earlier this year when his impatience for starting a family began to starkly conflict with my own ambitions. We were headed in completely different directions, Andy and I. Black clothes and burlesque corsets were not outfits he wanted on his domestic goddess.

You cut into my story. You were not someone who dwelt on irreconcilable differences between adults. The very mention of a family made you wrinkle your nose in distaste and I instantly liked you more for that. Suddenly you pulled a pen from your suit jacket and wrote something on a scrap of paper, then passed it to me. You wanted me to read it aloud. At first I felt sick – such an instruction ran in stark opposition to any way I was used to conducting myself. I flushed and swallowed nervously. You said I could whisper the words instead, for good practice.

'Sir, I would like to be spanked through my knickers until I come for you.' I almost fainted with excitement and apprehension but was so glad I finally got the words out that I grinned and giggled. You told me it was no laughing matter. You wanted it louder, and I promised I would do it later, when we were out of the restaurant.

Those words kept running through my mind, the anticipation building through the coffees and out onto the street in the crisp night air. I wanted you. I was ready for your touch between my legs and yearned to prove the extent of my desire. I displayed some impatience when you didn't immediately suggest we go to your place in Maida Vale. You were having no petulance. You grabbed my wrist firmly and pulled me into the alley that ran alongside the restaurant. I clacked behind you on my heels, careening unsteadily like an untethered vessel in a gale.

I was up against the brick wall before I could say anything, and you had captured the other arm so that both were pinned above me. Then my senses swirled in delight as you leaned into me and I felt you hard for the first time. You made me say the words again, louder, without humour, until I too was deadly serious about it, almost crying for it to happen there and then, over the cardboard boxes and oil canisters and without finesse. I wanted to be spanked and to come for you – but I burned for you to take control. Instead I was treated to a few exquisite seconds of your grown-up man's hands running over my satin knickers, and two fingers eased into my honey-soaked sex.

Our eyes met at this moment and sealed the deal: a spell made in the gutter that would take us both to heaven. You gently withdrew and sucked your fingers while I twisted into knots with the shame of bareing myself so completely for you, so soon. I lowered my head and you gently brushed my thick dark brown hair from my eyes, then led me sedately to the street where, to my total indignation, you hailed a cab and pressed a £20 note in my hand for the fare.

'I'll call you,' was all you said and, in my inebriated condition, I found myself being transported home, horny and giddy and desperate for more, incredulous of what had just happened. I kept telling myself you were a rare gentleman; you didn't want to take advantage of me. You were preparing me for something else. But after I was home, lying on my sofa with a toothmug of vodka, I began to think you'd turned me down. Those fateful words: 'I'll call you,' were not ones I'd learned from experience to be loaded with promise. I'd failed the test of what it took to be your playmate.

I was just about to indulge in some mindless late-night TV when my mobile rang.

'When I said I would call you, you didn't think we'd be discussing interest rates, did you, after all we've talked about tonight?'

'I don't know.' I giggled, feeling relief at hearing your voice. 'I thought you might have changed your mind and suddenly wanted to come home with me.'

'Oh, I want that more than anything. But there's

plenty of time. You have to learn a little discipline. You're eager, aren't you? But you are going to have to show me just how much.'

'How much? Couldn't you feel that for yourself?' I answered, sarcastically. Typical. I was impatient and immature. I needed that spanking!

'My sweet treasure, I know you're interested in me, but I'd like you to do something to prove it. Remember I told you what a nice voice you have? It's my thing, if you like, as being tied up is yours. And you would like me to tie you, wouldn't you? Take you to a hotel and bind you to the bed with handcuffs, stand over you and show it to you?'

'Yes.' I couldn't stand much more of his measured voice, saying the things I'd longed to hear for years.

'Oh, come on! Has the kitty got your little pink tongue? I want to hear you being honest about what you want. There's no one there with you, is there?'

'No.'

'Nor here. I'm all on my own in my apartment. I'm just settling down on the sofa and it's quiet. No one is going to disturb us for what we're about to do.'

'What can we do in separate locations?' Why was I acting so dumb when I knew what it was you wanted?

'You're a bright girl. What do you think?'

'You want me to say things to you... over the phone.'

'Correct.' You were playing with the intonation of patience, but you must have been as desperate for release as I was. You would be a good teacher.

'What do you want me to say?' I asked. I was dragging out the inevitable.

'I want you to say what you think a man like me might need to hear when he's so hard he's about to burst the zip of his trousers.'

'Is this what they call phone sex?'

'We haven't started yet. I want to know lots and lots of dirty details, because you know what I'll be doing, don't you?'

'And I'll be doing the same. I want you. I want to feel you punish me and fuck me. You felt how wet I was.'

'Ah, that's getting better... did I hear an F-word? What you want will come in good time. I keep telling you to be patient. Few girls your age have learned to delay gratification. Now *I* want to come... but in good time.'

Your emphasis on particular words and the thought of you touching yourself as you spoke to me was breathtaking. And I had done this to you. I really was going to masturbate along with you, but would it be enough? I unzipped my skirt and let it fall to the floor. I left on my hold-ups and shoes and lounged in my smart shirt as I eased my fingers under the soaking crotch of my knickers. I was too wet for the friction I needed, and swollen to an obscene degree. I had a wicked idea. I went to my bedroom to fetch a mirror back into the living room so I could make out I was performing for a camera. It was an instant confidence boost.

I liked it that you called me 'girl.' It would have annoyed me if it had come from my boss or a person from the 'real' world. Yet in this voluptuous arena of fantasy you could call me anything you liked, if it aided your desire. Tonight we had set in motion a high-octane dynamic. It was charged with elegance and followed a pattern of sophistication that I did not have a name for but had recognised in a dozen French movies. It was Catherine Deneuve in *Belle de Jour*; Simone Signoret in *Les Diaboliques*, and that unknown gamine in Clouzot's *Women in Chains*. Daughters of darkness, who can find their release only in that wonderful exchange of power. And now I was about to step out of my comfort zone and find myself uttering expletives into my own phone. But more than this, I had to be creative. I knew you didn't want a mere diatribe of filth. I was scanning my brain for how to begin when you suggested it.

'Tell me the story about the dirty-minded financial broker who goes for a walk in the woods.'

I knew you wanted to hear more about that

fantasy when I'd alluded to it over dinner. Your eyes had lit up. You were my very own big bad wolf. And you were about to blow my cosy house down.

I told you the story in the third person to surrender responsibility: a girl (me) in a tight pencil skirt and form-fitting white blouse and jacket is taking a short cut through a wooded area when she happens upon a car park used by swinging couples. You made me go into detail about the sound of her shoes on the gravel, and the way she cannot take big strides because of her skirt. A man and a woman get out of a car and ask her if she would like a lift. It is obvious they are up to something, but they are attractive and she agrees to go with them. She gets into the back of the car with the woman as the man drives to somewhere even more secluded. The woman then binds her arms behind her back and walks her into the woods where she is forced to kneel on the leaves of the forest floor. The woman is measured and unemotional as she points out little things about their willing victim that inflames their refined sense of erotic aesthetics. I do so want to be shown off to master who will take me. I let this detail slip and then you were the one to go breathless. I pictured you vividly, firmly caressing yourself.

The woman rips the girl's skirt, revealing her buttocks and sex to the man. He rubs his erection and I imagine you doing the same. In my head the imaginary narrative collides with the reality of what I know you are doing, and I feel possessed by my acute craving for cock-flesh. I rub myself through my knickers, watching my obscene reflection and telling you I am going to have to use a dildo on myself, to be filled. My fantasy girl is made to perform oral sex on the man while the woman whips her with a thin stick. Every now and then you stop me and ask me to repeat lines such as, 'She is desperate for someone to fuck you, even the woman, as the man forces himself into your mouth.'

'I like the way you say "force",' you cut in. 'I have been so lenient with you tonight. Next time we meet, you will know all about 'force.' Would you like to be fucked by a woman? I have a number of very attractive friends who could oblige.'

'No. I want to be fucked by you,' I replied, aching with the urgency of needing attention and becoming distracted by my reflection, as if it were a TV screen image of a porno film.

'I am very close to coming,' you said, 'but I want you to do it for me. I want you to tell me what things you are doing to yourself and how you feel. I am so hard in my trousers I will have to release myself or I will shoot off in them for you and that would be no good. I'm not the one who loses control.'

I let go of all inhibitions at that point. I was

prepared to go all the way for you and it was the perfect initiation into being brave. I determined that the next time we met I would impress you with my candor.

'I want you to rub yourself between my legs and shoot all over me, sir.' I said. 'I am fingering myself through my knickers because I am too wet to touch skin on skin. I'm sliding onto the floor and off the sofa, tensing my legs. I am still wearing the shoes; only my skirt has gone. Oh, God I want you to tie me. To whip me and fuck me.'

'Can I do that in front of other people? Show them what a hot little slut I've found?'

Before I knew what I was agreeing to, the molten ascent began. I watched myself in the mirror and wished that you could see me in the moment of ultimate pleasure, my teeth sparkling and my head thrown back, my hand now stilled yet strategically placed and my shoes dangerously potent with their heels so close to my sex. I usually remain silent as my orgasm hits me, but this time I managed to tell you what was happening. I felt bereft that I wasn't able to see the effect it had on you but, as the sensations calmed down, I realised that I had admitted to being a 'hot little slut,' and I smiled.

You thanked me and I was just wondering how we could possibly proceed into normal conversation when you took control. And what you said sent me into paroxysms of delight.

'Very soon I will take you shopping for shoes. We'll go to Sloane Street and you can try on as many pairs as you like.'

I thought back to earlier this year when Andy and I had gone shopping for walking boots. I looked at myself once more, dreaming of high boots and glittering evening sandals. How radically life had changed in so little time. And what adventures awaited a hot little slut and her older man, playing the favourite game.

Acknowledgements

Thanks to
all our collaborators.

www.agentprovocateur.com